Sonii Marie, a personality with the nature of a dreaming romantic, looking for balance in mundane everyday activities; made from the clay of pain and past experiences; ostentatious in her views and behavior.

A personality that balances on the scales of life. A woman living in her imaginary shell, listening but drawing her own conclusions; wanting to show the world that in order to win your own fight, you must first forge your sword, which you will mark with pain, suffering, and consequences, and then a smile will be born and your soul will be reborn.

Her motto is 'to see rainbows, you first have to survive the rain'.

Sonii Marie

A BOOK WITHOUT A TITLE

AUSTIN MACAULEY PUBLISHERS™

LONDON • CAMBRIDGE • NEW YORK • SHARJAH

Ordering Information
Quantity sales: Special discounts are available on quantity purchases by corporations, associations, and others. For details, contact the publisher at the address below.

Publisher's Cataloging-in-Publication data
Marie, Sonii
A Book Without a Title

ISBN 9798891553620 (Paperback)
ISBN 9798891553644 (ePub e-book)
ISBN 9798891553637 (Audiobook)

Library of Congress Control Number: 2023924607

www.austinmacauley.com/us

First Published 2024
Austin Macauley Publishers LLC
40 Wall Street, 33rd Floor, Suite 3302
New York, NY 10005
USA

mail-usa@austinmacauley.com
+1 (646) 5125767

No acknowledgments is probably not a bad solution… if I knew what I know now, I would never have let this happen, so there are no thanks for writing all this… because the pain has left me with nothing…

And even the shitty concept of hope dying last is out of place now… Hope is for fools.

That would be the easiest thing to write. But is it true? No. Thank you, each and every one of you. Thank you on behalf of every person who fell and got up. Thank you for the opportunity to write down everything that was most important in this story and what could have contributed to at least one person finding the meaning of life again. This is a milestone and a huge success. Because only those who do not fight do not fail, and those who have failed call it a success.

This is my own opinion on this thing called life. It is not easy, but it is very beautiful… And although hope is for fools, and although not everyone can live with it side by side, I want to believe that it exists. I want to believe that despite everything, it pulls us out of hell. First of all, we have to believe in it!

But is this really true? As for me, I still doubt too often…

Table of Contents

Confession

If you reach the end, I hope you'll find the title yourself. That it will lead you to where you've always been afraid to go.

Don't be afraid. Dreams are within your reach. You just sometimes have to fight harder for them.

I understand that you're feeling a lot of pain and that it has made you lose faith in gratitude and hope. It's okay to have these feelings and to express them. Sometimes, when we go through difficult experiences, it can be hard to see beyond the pain.

However, it's important to remember that healing and positive changes are possible, even if it may not feel like it right now. If you ever need someone to talk to or support, don't hesitate to reach out.

You close your eyes and slump lifelessly, you're filled with that thing called hope, hoping that it will all end soon and you'll never have to utter those banal and self-hostile words again. I won't give up.

Your skin feels every centimeter, experiencing how much relief fills every inch of your body, relief that all the shit of your life will suddenly disappear and you'll find yourself in the place best suited for you.

Is this supposed to be hell in this case? It doesn't matter, I'll take anything just to not have to fight anymore. This is the most amusing experience I could have given myself, someone who has always been terrified of water with all my might.

Now, I'm losing myself in it and closing the circle of my life. This is probably what they call the ability of double self-destruction.

We weren't prepared with trial runs when entering this world, we didn't have the opportunity to plan our lives, which is why a certain percentage of humanity lives in constant unhappiness, unable to see any light.

Seeing only darkness and gradually surrendering their hearts and souls to it, thinking they're giving their lives for salvation. I've been thinking about this all the time when those demons became such close friends with me, to the point where they became the defining aspect of each subsequent destructive day.

I loved them and never fought against them, or at least that's what I believed for most of my life.

In the standard of humanity, men are always portrayed in the light of evil shadows, as the source of all the evil in this world, all the crap that befalls all women, both married and unmarried.

Cases of alcoholism, addiction, or even trivial reasons like having a bad character. Forgive me, but it's one big misunderstanding. Will there be any woman confirming my words? Probably yes, when it comes to the part related to men, but will the part about women's imperfections also resonate with them? Probably not.

We are too proud to admit how much we are self-absorbed, egotistic, narcissistic, and easily prone to addictions, with imperfection strictly derived from Adam's rib and those never achievable expectations.

This is not a confession or even a presentation of women's flaws. It's a story that makes me aware of how often we are to blame for our own failures, tears, and dramas.

It shows our weaknesses and the great responsibility that weighs on many of us. It stems from a lack of hmm, motivation? To become fully independent women who act and live according to their own rules.

Women who can love unconditionally and also deflect sadness and hurt from themselves like a shield. We can't. We usually explain ourselves with a wounded heart. That's bullshit! I stood up, and each of us can too; it just takes a bit more time than we think.

I stood up stronger than ever in my life. but to say that I stood up alone would be a lie. I stood up because I found the light, or rather, romantically speaking, the light found me. It remained within me even when everything else faded away.

Do you feel like you're already at the bottom? Like the void of water has taken you to where you wanted so badly? I felt the same, even though the bottom gave me a strange sense that nothing worse could happen. And yet.

Helplessly surrendering to the abyss, in that very moment, I experienced something they might call a freeze-frame of my life, when you suddenly see your whole life with its smallest, sometimes least significant elements.

As if it wasn't enough for you to remember how bad it was when you were conscious of it, now you fucking have to see it too.

Slide One

You scream, you scream, and you can't stop. The world spins and then stands still, the world spins and then stands still; a million endless times. You don't move, but you scream, and the scream slowly turns into a squeal, transitioning into a plea.

And that's when you hear it. You know it's not possible to hear, but the voice is so clear, so familiar, and brings relief amid all the screaming. The voice tries once again, in a mocking yet strangely comforting way, to remind you that there are no farewells, only love remains, that you don't see the wind but you feel it.

You'll see it. The voice becomes quieter, but you still hear it, as your scream releases its final breath, not signifying that you've stopped screaming. It's just that the scream is now with you always; when you close your eyes, when you sleep, and even when you perform the most mundane actions in your life.

It has become your best friend, and you've learned to live with it so well, learned to punish yourself so much, that you don't even know when to stop and return to living.

It's been six years already. So many damn years or perhaps just enough years to finally forgive myself. A beautiful summer day, so beautiful that you feel every ray of sunshine embracing your skin and the wind swirling around with unimaginable speed.

This day, hauntingly aware that it will be the last day for a long time when I felt the beauty of it all, the beauty of life.

The road was practically empty and wide as two people who have known each other forever and understood each other without words, baring the truth of life, embracing their greatest flaws, extreme emotions, secrets, trusting each other unconditionally, raced at a speed unknown to an ordinary mortal.

A friend who never leaves in moments of great fear, in moments of despair as well as great joy, a known and safe oasis forever. Forever. One big mess, there's no such thing as forever, there is only now, and this moment is where we must extract the most. Why?

Because he left her, at a time when she least expected it, at a time when they were doing what they loved, at a moment that brought them solace, where it was just the two of them and their thoughts, often separate, but it was their moment of escape and refuge. In their own little lost yet secure world where everything brought relief and bliss, he left her.

She stood there, screaming and waving her arms for help, but in vain. She suffered greatly and was filled with anger, unable to understand for a moment what had truly happened.

She stood frozen, awakening and breaking free from her stupor. Those were seconds of terrifying, the worst events of her life. She looked at the two parts of the smoking engine, searching for him, her best friend who was torn away from her life so suddenly.

Her eyes witnessed something they never wanted to see, but fear didn't paralyze her. It only fueled her because deep within her, a spark of hope still flickered, whispering, "Maybe, just maybe."

But no, when she saw the last flame extinguish, as she removed the helmet from his head, she knew. She simply knew. The lifeless body, torn apart inside the suit, became light as a feather, something she could lift.

Her hands fell lifelessly as she tried, time and time again, to wake him up, making it all feel like one fucking joke. With all her strength, she tried to put him back together, pushing everyone away, attempting to piece him together like a paper airplane.

The smell of blood was so intense it made her dizzy. It was as if that sarcastic bitch called Death had arrived. She stood there, laughing with all her might at how easily she had fulfilled her plan, and at her, the girl who was unprepared to witness the wreckage of life, a life so perfect yet so deeply unfathomable.

The laughter that surrounded her from every direction was no longer as loud, not even the screams she let out could drown out that voice, a voice that would probably be her companion for the rest of her life.

His eyes still looked, but there was no life in them anymore, it had departed, taking her life with it. In that very moment, she felt them rise together and depart, only they didn't go to the same place. not anymore.

She didn't leave him even for a moment. She knew, well, I'm quite certain she knew, but a fragment of awareness remained, a belief that just as he had been with her throughout her life, she would be by his side until the end of his.

Holding his hand in her hands, gently caressing his lifeless head, she waited. Waiting for a miracle? No, she was waiting for time to rewind, or waiting for him to open his eyes, silently pleading for just one nightmare of this night.

Unfortunately, she was waiting for the whole circus to arrive, the circus of hopeless human callousness, packing his body into a black bag, as if he were no longer human.

Hearing the voice of some despicable person, saying they had been summoned again to collect the pieces, she had the urge to turn him into one large piece of meat, ready to be devoured by starved wolves, screaming, "I'm here, you hopeless human."

She couldn't even remember how his face looked when she said that; she was too consumed with arranging his lifeless body to ensure the most comfortable journey to wherever they were taking him before.

Hours spent in a place where the stench of death could be sensed from miles away, accompanied by that laughter, the same laughter that delighted in its sick collection of conquests, were torture.

The torture was hazy, but it permeated every inch of her body, which, in a strange way, still believed that it was all one grand fiction, one grand theatrical performance.

However, the figure of the rushing woman interrupted her thoughts, pulling her away from every thought she didn't want to entertain in her mind. She realized then that it wasn't some damn dream, that it wasn't over, she understood that it was just beginning and probably would never end.

It was at that moment, consciously or unconsciously, that she reached out her hand and allowed herself to be swallowed by the abyss. And the price for the opportunity to be drawn into endless sadness, grief, and guilt was punishment.

It was like metaphorically placing upon herself her own crown of thorns, which, whenever she saw a chance for self-forgiveness, reminded her that she couldn't. That the pain was meant to endure, that the sense of guilt wasn't a hazy memory that could be set aside and move on.

Days were passing, and everything inside her was intensifying. Helplessness and a sense of responsibility for those events caused her to retreat to a place where it would be most comfortable for her to internally kill herself.

She doesn't even remember the day she bid him farewell for the last time; the hazy memories of screeching fire truck sirens are so unclear that even after years, it's difficult for her to determine if they were actually there in that moment.

She felt trapped in a closed circle, something she couldn't comprehend. It was a pure abstraction happening before the eyes of hundreds of people who participated, as it's nicely called, in the final journey.

Could it be that her lack of memories, when she should have had them, was the result of so many people, so many doctors trying to keep her in the best possible mental condition to attend and not understand?

The amount of crap they pumped into her would be enough to bring down a horse. but not her, her consciousness continued to replay second by second that day, the day when they both died.

They both coped in different ways. Escape became her defense, and the lethargy in which her mind could shut off. But no amount of alcohol and all those pills helped her get rid of the images swirling in her head.

It only made sure that no one expected normal functioning from her anymore, allowing her to experience loss and grief in the way she deemed best. After many attempts to reason with her lost sanity, which always ended in the same repetitive pattern, briefly pulling her out of the cursed vortex.

Glasses and everything else that was usually within her reach, whether half-empty remnants of vodka or beloved vases and plates of food placed on the small table in her bedroom every day for over two months, hoping she might eat.

Everything eventually landed on the floor, causing considerable damage. All the holes in the floor, still present in her home to this day, serve as a reminder or rather prevent her from forgetting that she found her way through hell.

They both coped in different ways… Escape became her defense, and the lethargy in which her mind could shut off. But no amount of alcohol and all those pills helped her get rid of the images swirling in her head. It only made sure that no one expected normal functioning from her anymore, allowing her to experience loss and grief in the way she deemed best. After many attempts to reason with her lost sanity, which always ended in the same repetitive pattern… briefly pulling her out of the cursed vortex. Glasses and everything else that was usually within her reach, whether half-empty remnants of vodka or beloved vases and plates of food placed on the small table in her bedroom every day for over two months, hoping she might eat. Everything eventually landed on the floor, causing considerable damage. All the holes in the floor, still present in her home to this day, serve as a reminder or rather prevent her from forgetting that she found her way through hell.

Weeks passed, and each day looked essentially the same. It was unclear to her whether it was day or still night, and it didn't matter much. What truly mattered were the repetitive patterns that had been going on for so many weeks.

Building and constructing a wall, brick by brick, to keep everyone out, surrounding herself with a moat so that she would never feel anything again. She wanted to feel only emptiness and guilt.

The assistance in achieving this goal came from her best friends, in the form of small white sweetly shimmering pills, washed down with whatever burned her throat the most. It was a new reality for her, one that, like an understanding life partner, had organized itself and adapted to the new rules in place. The rules that would hold, for now.

She couldn't even remember exactly how much time had passed, but certainly not enough, because her angelic guard still hadn't left her apartment.

When she decided, probably for the first time in a long while, to see the wreckage in her apartment—or rather, not see it, simply to get out of bed—she experienced that piercing pain that, despite considering her well-being and constant self-contempt, made her want to believe that her body was finally integrating with her mind and would never let her forget.

But we know how unpredictable life can be, or rather, she knew it better than anyone in her closest surroundings. She saw that the looks she received were crushing, and in the distance, she could only hear.

"Call an ambulance!" It was her beloved father, who, like no one else in the world, tried not to judge her, having some incomprehensible pact with her best friend, staying by her side.

"Call an ambulance!" Her father's voice echoed throughout her apartment, as her best friend or mother finally wiped away their shock and reached for that damn phone.

She stood between the bedroom and the bathroom, looking, just looking. As the stain on the floor grew larger, unaware of when she collapsed to the ground, saying, "Finally."

Did she think her suffering was finally ending? Probably, if not for one small detail. She didn't hear that sarcastic laughter that should have accompanied her then.

She isn't quite sure how much time passed as she opened her eyes and saw an unfamiliar space surrounding her. The brightness with its vivid yellow hurt her eyes, and in her mind, she asked herself, why?

It wasn't a religious heaven or hell, nothing like that. After all, that would be too beautiful to be real, and she had long stopped believing in miracles.

It was just an ordinary, poor hospital room, where all she could sense was the smell of everything that triggers the worst nauseating reflexes in a person.

She heard only one thing as she looked around the room, searching for answers, any answers. She only heard one voice.

"Now, you have someone to live for."

She thought it was some fucking joke, that she was hearing voices again, that in the moment when she wondered why she couldn't just leave when she desired it so much, she heard the voice.

Suddenly, she felt a touch on her hand, the hand that seemed to be filled with every possible amount of needles with thin strings through which something was entering her already depleted body.

It was her father. He said in a quiet voice, "Now, you have someone to live for, you must."

He looked at her with glassy eyes, filled with compassion and at the same time, an unfathomable joy and hope that she couldn't decipher.

She didn't understand any of it. She looked at him, or rather in his direction, but the image was blurred, too blurred to see what she was bestowed with and what she considered the greatest punishment during her childhood. Colors.

But the colors disappeared, disappeared at the moment when she tried to shape her body like a paper toy, not long ago, yet further and further in time.

She has been sleeping for over ten hours, according to the people gathered in her new hotel room, uh hospital room. The doctor said it's good because she needs to regain strength.

"We don't know when she last slept."

"Oh God, give her strength."

She heard the conversation of those people, but her eyelids were so heavy that she couldn't open them to see who was talking to whom. The voices were unrecognizable because the noise and ringing in her ears kept drowning everything out.

"I'm here, darling," her father said. She knew it was her father because his voice was non-judgmental and full of concern.

"You'll manage, you'll find a way to get up, and the price doesn't matter. You have a new life within you now, and it's still there after everything. It's strong, and so are you, you just don't know it yet. You have someone to live for."

Is she dreaming? What does all this mean? What are these words? Did she unknowingly swallow a magical ball filled with life? Will she be able to live as she did before? She opens her eyes and looks at her father without saying a word.

"Rather a girl," he says.

She continues to look at him with lifeless eyes, trying to make sense of it all, but she can't for the life of her.

"The beginning of the fourth month." Her father's words trail off.

"This can't be true!" She screams internally to herself—this can't be happening for real. What have I done for someone to play such cruel jokes on me?

"Then everything comes back to her, everything seems to make some sense, or maybe in that one moment after so many months, she's able to piece together her thoughts a little and extract the facts from them."

"Yes, around the fourth month before all of this happened, I had a best friend, and I had someone whom I thought I wanted to build my life with. But even then, fate mocked me when I saw with my own eyes how a person close to me spent intimate time with my own cousin."

"She repeated it to herself several times in her mind as she continued to gather her thoughts."

Then she felt hurt and deceived like never before, but the strength of her character didn't allow her to feel broken, only an immense desire to escape.

Where and with whom to escape when there's a problem? She quickly dialed the number to her refuge, which, as usual in life, was there for her when she needed it the most.

"The sea?" He asked her.

"The sea!" She replied without giving herself a moment to think.

Living in that moment, they did something they both loved most in the world. Riding a motorcycle was a passion in itself, and only a few could taste the adrenaline that drives it, understanding the feelings it can evoke, the fear one should truly have.

Two people supporting each other their whole lives, arguing over the smallest differences in opinions, capable of discarding everything just to extend a helping hand and pull the other to the surface during any problems.

That one moment took everything away from them. His wife, a husband and a father of two daughters, and hers, the light. Because if angels were to descend to Earth and perform miracles, her best friend was such an angel, summoned back too soon.

Leaving only pain, suffering, memories, and the repeated words, love remains. You will see, deeply rooted in the darkness.

Slide Two

During the moments when her entire world had been turned upside down, she faced a challenge she couldn't share with anyone. There was no one left to turn to, so she had to learn to make decisions on her own, knowing that support wouldn't come.

The following months were an absolute torment, and she didn't know how to cope or what the future held. Not long ago, she had lost her older brother, and now she had to become a mother.

Life's irony laughed in her face, until the moment she felt the first movement of the tiny being inside her, as if saying, "I'm here, Mom—hold on."

I wish I could say everything changed at that moment, but the truth is that she had to painfully learn to navigate a path that had been unknown to her for the past four months. She had to endure and figure out what came next.

Pregnancy didn't turn out to be the most beautiful experience of her life, as it's often said to be for expectant mothers. Perhaps it was the result of how the initial weeks had unfolded, reportedly the most crucial for the baby's development.

Those were the weeks when all she could do was take as much of everything as possible, just to make the pain and guilt disappear, even if only for a brief moment.

Until the final day of that condition, the tiny being was kept under constant care, while she, well, she was more under supervision to prevent her from making another unforgivable mistake.

The first gusts of spring wind heralded the arrival of that little but extraordinary creature, descending from a soft, white cloud into this dreadful world—a little miracle that yearned to live despite everything it was exposed to in the early moments of its small existence.

It would be a lie to say it was effortless, knowing that she had already taken one life, she had to pay for it once again. The 72 hours felt like an eternity, and the pain that accompanied it was incomparable to how much she wanted to feel it, how much she wanted to punish herself.

The sheer amount of aids to help bring the little being into the world could probably knock down a horse, colloquially speaking. And even though it might seem that the best solution would be to simply extract it from the mother's womb, the chances were close to zero.

Her body was so weakened and depleted, her heart refusing to cooperate, her breath faltering, and on top of it all, her blood failing to support.

It gave her a silent signal that either she would endure this or the innocent creature wouldn't have a chance to experience anything beyond her. Whatever kind of mother she could be?

Multiple cardiac arrests, thousands of blows to the face to bring her back and make her breathe were nothing because in her mind, there was only one word echoing. "Fight, I'm here."

And although she felt lonely and abandoned, in reality, her father and the second-best person who surrounded her with care she didn't truly deserve were there with her, repeating like a mantra, "You can do it, you can do it."

She did it! Even though she spent another week in the intensive care unit, she did it! The days were an endless torment because she longed to see that little monster who had forced her into a battle she wasn't prepared to fight.

Then it happened, something that not even the devil himself would expect in his worst nightmares, but she had already surrendered her soul. He appeared.

The father of that little being, who should never have returned, but who was welcomed with open arms. The vision of promises made by her bedside blurred the last remnants of consciousness she had regained.

She knew it would be better, that she needed help for this innocent child to experience happiness because her happiness no longer mattered; it was buried along with everything that gave meaning to her life.

"I have changed, I understand, I regret. I will fix it."

All those delusions spoken in the most beautiful tone a human can produce.

She believed. She wanted to believe so much. Her eyes welled up with tears as she finally saw her. The little girl who resembled her so much from the first days of her life.

Her velvety skin trembled as a hand reached out to gently touch her. In that moment, she wasn't ready to do anything more. Everything seemed so unreal yet so undeniably true.

It was her father who, without giving her a choice or the right to refuse, placed the little creature on her bed, helping to arrange the most comfortable position for both of them.

The ice was broken in a strange, mystical way, and even though she remained motionless with countless things attached to her body to keep her alive, she didn't give up.

In that moment, she did everything she could to kiss her on the forehead with her cracked lips and whisper, "You're probably my miracle, and I'm your mother. We'll make it."

She looked at her father and his glassy eyes, where perhaps for the first time in many months, there was not just hope, which he probably always had, but relief because his little daughter found a faint glimmer of strength to fight through the ruins.

She looked at her, mesmerized, as her own little miracle, touched by her fingertips, smiled back at her. In a hoarse, soft voice, the little one said, "Daddy, I think she likes me. She knows it's me."

The eyes of her father and her friend, who had been by her hospital bed all along, burst into laughter together.

"She loves you, and she lives for you. And you have to live for her, understand?" They said.

She nodded her head, feeling the tear rolling down onto the tiny head of her little miracle. After a few weeks, they left the hospital, leaving behind walls filled with pain and walls filled with joy, walls that witnessed so many wonders of life that it would take more than one generation to comprehend.

He was with them, she let him into her life, into a different life, hoping that it wasn't just a dream, all those words, all those promises. But.

The first hours in her apartment, the first moments that should have been the most beautiful, the ones she could have told the little being about as it grew up, turned out to be the beginning and the end of a dream from which she was abruptly awakened.

Sore, exhausted, stitched up with countless sutures, all she longed for was freedom to learn how to take care of her, to anticipate her needs without words.

However, the sensations of 72 hours of labor and weeks spent in intensive therapy took a toll on her just a few hours after returning home, where, despite promises, she was left to fend for herself.

Too weak to ask, scream, or even beg for help, she accepted what was offered to her. Transportation home with her little child, assistance in climbing the stairs, and that was it. He had brought many of his things to her apartment, but she only saw him three days later.

She forgave, even though an overwhelming sense of helplessness grew within her when her daughter cried in the crib on the first night, and she couldn't get up, no matter how hard she tried, calling, whispering to her, "Just a little longer, Mommy will get up soon."

Hours seemed to pass until she finally managed to rise, gather the last of her strength, and lift the little one from the crib to comfort her and whisper how much she meant to her, begging for forgiveness for what she had put her through. From that day on, they slept together.

On the third day, when he appeared in her home, her own home, he treated her as if she were nobody. and her home, her sanctuary, which had never judged her, felt like a hotel. He left.

The following days were immersed in both physical pain and an incredible love that began to bloom within her as they spent every day and night together, when that little being became her confidant, and she told her all the stories.

She lost count of how many days had passed since they were home. On another day, a terrible crash and noise woke her up from sleep. There was banging on the door and shouts. It was then, for the first time, that she felt the need to protect that little being because she didn't really know what was happening.

Without much thought, she jumped out of bed and ran to the front door, opening it. She saw him stumbling into the house. The one who had promised. It was also the first time he struck her, a blow to her face, and the stinging and redness on her face were nothing compared to the pain she felt moments after he forcefully threw her against the wall.

Everything that reminded her of the torture, the hours of suffering she endured to bring her beloved daughter into the world, was shattered. She never asked for help, and she didn't want any more mercy, but she was so afraid for her little daughter. She managed to call for help.

Her father was there so quickly that she hadn't even crawled to the room where her little princess was peacefully sleeping. His words were so distant from her that she could barely hear them.

When she opened her eyes, everything seemed so familiar, so homely or were hospital rooms now a second home?

She spent another month in the confines of her sanctuary apartment, taking care of her daughter as best as she could, given the circumstances. She observed how her loved ones cared for her daughter and for her, never leaving her alone, day or night.

She knew, only then did she truly understand, that despite everything, they wouldn't let her be alone. Yet, she was a master at making decisions that led her toward self-destruction.

Once again, she forgave. She stayed with him for the next two years of their little daughter's life, enduring and accepting everything. Enduring everything, but for what exactly? Was there someone else?

Bullshit once again, she punished herself and unquestioningly, always justifying her reasons in the name of other people's opinions. Or maybe deep down, she wanted to please the woman who gave birth to her? She wanted a sense of appreciation and the feeling that her mother could also be proud of her?

But she had already sentenced her a long time ago, contributing to another of the most self-destructive decisions in her life. She forced her to legalize a relationship with a man who was the father of her little miracle but also her tormentor.

A man who exploited her sense of guilt and fragile mental state to make her feel worthless or rather, worth nothing.

After months of deception and fabricating the greatest amount of nonsense possible, she finally had no choice but to open the door and see. Her mother, his mother, the man she had to bury, the one she left in the middle of the road, whose voice in her head still screams, denying her respite.

A woman so honest, so genuine, and so loving toward her, as if she were her own mother, a mother who never judged her or yelled in her face about how terrible a person she was and how it was her fault for what happened, bringing shame to the family and slowly killing her own father—unlike her own mother.

This woman, the mother of her friend, openly expressed that she was angry, not angry about what happened, but about how lost she had become, how she allowed herself to lose her sense of self and self-worth.

She gave her a reason not to attend the wedding, which deep down she believed to be a mistake. In fact, everyone, including herself, knew it was a mistake that would be difficult for her to escape from.

However, on that day, she said something that made a small part of her desired something else. She needed to know that even though he was gone, he still existed and spoke to her with his mother's voice, but he spoke.

What strength does one need or how much love must one have to tell their own child, who was buried, that despite the heart being torn apart, there remains knowledge, knowledge stronger than anything, that he left while doing what he loved the most, and that the person who was with him at that time was also his miracle.

That miracle was her, the girl who, if given the choice to give her life for something or someone she loves, would do so without hesitation and be ready for everything. Because she is one of the few people in the world who, when she gives her heart, gives it forever.

She said enough. "Leave and take your things," she finally told him, knowing the consequences it would bring. It was a moment that became her new battle, a fight for a new day and something she had yet to comprehend. She had no idea that when she made the decision, daring to take the final blow directed at her, deep down she knew it would bring some sense of purpose.

The easiest solution turned out to be building a wall. A wall that became her knight, shielding her from all the world's emotions. She shut off her humanity to feel nothing, only striving to find her own path.

Home, her sanctuary, was the only place where she could remove her mask and show her emotions, the opportunity to hold love in her heart, but love only for her daughter and those closest to her who were always by her side. The rest ceased to matter to her—they existed, they lived, and that was all.

No one will break her anymore. She tried to rise and live with that belief, compartmentalizing all the memories and negative events of her life that stripped away her sense of self-worth. Then, she remembered her childhood.

If she had the awareness back then that she has now, she would interpret it differently, not listening to her parents saying that everything happens for a reason. That she was marked by God in a special way for a purpose.

For what purpose? Perhaps only to be a martyr of the world and endure everything so that nothing would happen to others.

"Childhood," she uttered, closing her eyes.

Slide Three

Is it worth reminiscing about something that supposedly never happened? Her childhood, which she only vaguely remembers, didn't resemble happy events that influenced her entire later life. Although one thing was true. It did have an impact on her later life, even though she didn't realize it back then.

From a very young age, she was filled with shame and a sense of rejection. She always knew she was never meant to be in this world, and when she was here, her existence only reminded everyone of tragic family events.

She could never adapt to everyday situations, living in her own world since she can remember, a world of imaginary friends and fairy tale-like stories.

Days and years went by, and she increasingly resembled a loner, despite maintaining contact with many people, deep down feeling a constant lack of self-acceptance and shame.

The early years of her life were erased from her memory, probably because there was nothing particularly memorable about them. However, the memories from the day of the accident are still very vivid in her mind because that day marked not only a psychological but, most importantly, a physical transformation.

Car accidents are quite common events that take something away or give something in return. Some people strongly feel the need to change their lives, claiming that in some inexplicable way, they have been given a second chance by fate.

However, I believe that the fear that enveloped them at that time left such a strong mark that, just like half of humanity fears the road to heaven or hell, whatever truly exists, it is no miracle but rather a plain, damn piercing fear.

However, she was not afraid; she always took care of everyone except herself. Her parents were the most important to her at that time. It was their well-being that mattered, not hers.

Her mother, overwhelmed by the contradictions of her own inner voice, forced to make a decision that no one should have to make. No one should choose and decide on the worth of love, to prioritize one over the other.

When the fire brigade arrived at the scene and she was the only one able to freely escape the crushed vehicle, she shouted to save her family, fully aware that the choice had to be made now, that every decision she made would impact not only her family's future but also her daughter's.

Every element came together as a whole. She couldn't choose, couldn't decide, unable to bear the burden of human existence, still believing that everything would turn out fine and both of them would come out unharmed from this situation.

The strength of a mother's love knows no bounds; the word unconditional took on a deeper, profound meaning.

Her father loved her more than anything in the world and always told her she was his little princess and the apple of his eye. Their relationship was stronger than the average father–daughter relationship because the word father evoked a repulsive reaction in her.

It was he who said that if someone tried to help him without first prioritizing the safety of his little daughter, things would get really unpleasant. Perhaps in other circumstances, the person closest and most accessible would be prioritized, but that day they helped her first.

Both of them were safe, and the embrace of her father and mother brought a soothing relief that, in the face of death's merciless gaze, worked miracles in that moment.

The adrenaline that accompanied the accident slowly started to regulate and calm down, and the effects began to make themselves known. In reality, she wasn't trapped in the car wreck; it was her trapped leg that made any movement impossible.

Verdict. Amputation.

A teenage child doesn't understand such words, and they probably don't comprehend the consequences and everything that follows. They simply accept everything because, in essence, they have no voice or say in the matter. They are still at an age when someone else makes decisions about their life.

"No," her mother's voice sounded.

"Never in my life," her father said, raising his voice toward both the mother and the doctor. "Anything but that. There must be some other option, another chance, anything." His voice trembled.

The doctor's unreadable gaze revealed nothing. "Very well," they replied.

The surgery lasted for several hours, and it had to be repeated five more times to determine the outcome of all attempts to salvage what shouldn't have been saved.

"We can't do anything more, but it's still more than we expected," the doctor explained.

"What now?" She asked.

"Heavy and lengthy rehabilitation," they replied.

"Thank you. It means a lot. I'm so grateful for this uneven battle. Now, it's my turn," her father responded.

You may wonder what remained from the wreckage of the crushed leg. Apart from forty scars and a visible defect, a small portion of muscle in the lower part of the calf was saved.

Years of learning to regain health and, most importantly, full functionality followed. Her father was a man with a big heart, channeling all his energy and passion into the goal that became his life's purpose.

Sharing his life with a woman who carried all the surrounding sadness in her heart gave him the strength to fight for what mattered most to them. She had to regain full functionality, to run and jump again, and as she grew older, she had to feel like a fully valued woman in simple moments, like wearing high-heeled shoes.

He fought fiercely, inventing new devices to facilitate her full rehabilitation, even selling half of their apartment against his wife's dissatisfaction just to obtain the funds needed to cover the costs associated with building various equipment. Despite the tough times in their home, he never gave up, explaining that the price was worth it all.

He believed in it with all his might, and his dreams finally began to yield results as he had planned in his mind.

After many months, he witnessed firsthand the changes and progress his little daughter was making. His happiness fueled him even more.

He became a symbol not only of his honor in fighting and his daughter's recovery but also a role model to emulate, spoken of with clear excitement in people's voices.

The matter grew to such a scale that the doctors who fought to save his daughter's limb, with his consent and based on his actions, wrote and developed special rehabilitation techniques that were implemented for daily use nationwide.

It was the power of love that drove him so passionately. She emerged from it practically unscathed, with only visual imperfections that, with the advancements in medicine over the years, she managed to improve, so that the reminder of it could be minimized for her or anyone else.

However, internally, it still lowered her self-esteem and sense of self-worth, even though she tried with all her might to forcefully expel those feelings from within her. But every small situation reminded her of it—going to the swimming pool, the beach, or even wanting to wear a dress, which had been foreign to her for many years.

It wasn't self-pity she sought for herself—it was more of a lack of self-assurance, the fear that anyone who wanted to harm her could use it against her. But she lived, she danced, and she embraced being a woman. Although she always knew that if she were with someone, it would bring a kind of aversion.

She lived with it, and even though she was filled with questions of why it had happened to her specifically, she was grateful for who she was. The relationship between her and her parents could often be described as tense but compassionate.

Her father always spoke the truth, capable of exposing his own weaknesses. His eternal understanding and perpetual concern filled her with pride, not only in herself but also in the environment she was surrounded by at that time.

She had no shame in making late-night phone calls to her dad, making countless requests for support and pick-ups from places she needed to be. All of these interactions only reinforced her sense of importance.

Her mother, though life wasn't always easy for her, she would sometimes, in her own twisted way, show love and support, even if it meant causing pain with her bitter and cutting words.

Their wisdom and years of experience, the moments of trial they faced, shaped in her a sense of strong independence and a strong voice for her own rights and opinions, even if they weren't always right, but always driven by the freedom to express her thoughts.

What more could one ask for? Perhaps only for the world to hear about them and learn from their example, to understand what true conscious parenting means.

Deep Breath

These are just glimpses of her life that have always accompanied her in moments of sadness and happiness. What truly happened later was both the best and the worst thing that could have happened to her.

It's important to clarify one thing from the beginning—it's not that she suffered her whole life. Suffering was her destiny, but the sun often managed to break through the gloomy clouds.

However, this is the story of her life, a tale of survival and finding purpose. A small glimmer of hope she could hold onto and live, live the way she always wanted to, as described in all those books she had the opportunity to read throughout her life.

To make the human quotes about happiness and fulfilling dreams not just empty words spoken by everyone but to make them true. To make the miracle happen if you believe in it with all your heart.

Imagine. Close your eyes.

The depth, a black abyss, and from it emerges a black figure, completely covered in tar, dripping, crawling. It surfaces, slowly approaching, reaching out a hand, as the tar flows and drips onto the floor.

The air becomes heavy, transforming into a dense odor. The stench of suffering intensifies, only to witness something truly unbelievable. The crawling human piece rises, and with each subsequent drop of dripping tar falling to the ground, it transforms into a glistening tear.

The colors start to shift, gradually resembling a rainbow. The image begins to swirl, and deep down, you can't believe what you're witnessing. A familiar figure takes on a known form.

You start to hear sounds, attempting to align them with the image unfolding before your eyes. Sweat drips down your forehead, and your heart starts playing a rapid, melodic tune. You question whether you've simply lost your mind.

Do you think about when you will wake up?

Now she stands before you, her skin glistening, her eyes shining, illuminating the room you're in. Her smile pierces you to the core. You have never seen anything more beautiful. It is in your eyes that she has taken the form she had kept hidden within herself all these years.

She found herself. It was you who broke down the walls surrounding her heart, who found a crack to get through. It was thanks to you that she became a butterfly and yearned to fly.

It was because of you that she experienced the most beautiful moments, capturing them in the silent words of her soul. You awakened her from the slumber she was trapped in. You gave her the strength she had lost along the way.

It was you who taught her what love is. Love at first sight, how it permeates you, and yet you allow it without guarding your safe world. You showed her the light and taught her how to follow it.

It was you who showed her the pain of losing true love, leaving behind a glimmer of hope.

Slide Four

Have you ever wondered what love truly is and how to recognize it? I'm sure many have heard this question along with various answers. However, in my opinion, one must truly experience something extraordinary, profound, and have it, and then lose it, to be certain, essentially to distinguish infatuation from love.

Knowing all this and living through it, everyone would probably say that they won't make the same mistake again, that they've learned their lesson that they want to fix everything. But will they succeed?

Her story was different, yet so similar to many others. Only small details remained different. Two people, her and him, love, end of story. But not this time. Even though the circumstances of their meeting were written in a rather novel-like way.

And the question arises, if she could turn back time, would she not go to that place to meet him? Would it be better not to give him a chance to experience love at first sight and fight for what the world placed before them?

Despite everything, she would do it all over again, fully aware, and she wouldn't turn around if given another chance. It was him who taught her everything.

It was a beautiful day in May, and the sun had been making its presence known since the early morning, knocking on every room it could find a crack in, as an uninvited guest, to bless everyone with its beauty.

On that day, she seemed different too. Calmer than usual, despite the overwhelming responsibilities that awaited her every day. Her little being was already over three years old, which made each day so different from the previous one.

She poured all her energy into raising her to be the best person in the world, assuring her that her love for her was boundless despite the difficult start they both had. She lived solely for her, endlessly devoted.

She filled the missing pieces of her soul, leaving only one free, a sacred place untouched by thick mystical walls that no one would ever breach. She changed her entire life, keeping only those people by her side who couldn't hurt her and those who would never remind her of the past.

She didn't judge and didn't force herself to make the decision to forgive because forgiveness was the one thing she couldn't do for herself. It was her scar that was meant to stay with her forever, and she had to befriend it and learn to live with it.

She lived, filled with household and professional responsibilities, simply being a mother, hoping to be the best mother in the world, ensuring that her daughter would never experience from her hands, words, and actions what she had experienced as a helpless little girl.

She didn't try to build a life for herself, didn't need support or a man's arm. She became self-sufficient and independent, armed to protect herself from harm. She simply became numb to other people, as cold as a rock. Leaving her home, her sanctuary, her heart became covered in thick ice.

On that day, it was not meant to be any different. A simple outing with her old friends to accompany her on what is commonly called the final journey in her maiden status, if you know what I mean.

The party was arranged, the girls were summoned, and childcare was taken care of. The standard set of black outfits was prepared, with perhaps a small exception—on that day, high-heeled shoes were meant to reign. Well, why not?

Due to avoiding any kind of social interaction for so many months, she agreed to be the so-called bait for a surprise meeting. She made a call to arrange a standard beer because of such a long absence, choosing a place other than the roadside bar where they usually used to meet.

The clock struck nine, and she arrived at the meeting place punctually, ordering two beers and waiting for the person who was accustomed to being late because something extraordinary always had to happen.

After a few minutes of waiting, they were sitting together, starting an awkward conversation because what could they talk about after so many years and months where contact was minimal, barely surpassing the question, "How have you been?"

They had been sitting for a while, and she had an irresistible feeling that she didn't really want to be in this place. The rescue came shortly after she finished asking herself how much longer.

Squeals and shouts brightened up the place where they both found themselves at that moment, and the future bride kept exclaiming, "I knew it, I knew it!" in an attempt to avoid an awkward situation.

Perhaps nobody mentioned how utterly strange it was that she called to ask for a beer just two weeks before her wedding to 'refresh the relationship' and make things less awkward at her own wedding.

One of the girls immediately reached into her big bag and pulled out a whole set of accessories that accompany such occasions; headbands, sashes, and other disgustingly pink things.

But hey, she whispered to her best friend, who was immensely happy about the prospect of going out together like in the old days.

She had stood by her side for so many years, witnessed and heard things that could be deemed breathtakingly horrifying, written under the influence of intoxicants, yet she never judged—she simply was. So, how could she ruin her friend's happiness now?

The taxi arrived, taking along six slightly tipsy girls dressed in Halloween-like outfits (laughter). They applied makeup on the way to their destination and discreetly sipped smuggled alcohol from their purses, behaving like teenagers allowed to stay out longer than curfew for the first time in their lives.

The journey passed quickly, and they briskly walked along the city's most lively street, aiming to find an available table where they could surrender themselves to further revelry.

They were relieved to discover that it had been so long since they went out together that they didn't even realize that at such an early hour, practically all the tables in that place were free, and the real party magic didn't start until around midnight.

They laughed, drank, and playfully interacted with random people for the sake of fun and, more specifically, for the future bride to complete various tasks assigned to her on this night.

They danced with strangers in the middle of the crowded street, charmed people into buying them drinks, and engaged in various playful contests that were meant to lighten their evening.

At one point, while performing one of the tasks, they encountered a man who willingly agreed to buy drinks for the entire table if the girls agreed to let his group of friends join them.

The response came surprisingly quickly, probably due to the inhuman amounts of alcohol already consumed rather than sound judgment.

However, unlike the other girls, she couldn't feel at ease, and it wasn't necessarily due to the number of unfamiliar faces. It was because, at that moment, she saw something that had eluded her eyes for so long.

Colors, the entire palette of colors, became vividly saturated. Interweaving shades of red, orange, glassy piercing violet with a tinge of green, all surrounded by a black, charred burst of colorlessness.

The dark color, repulsive and always unsettling, pushed through more and more strongly, leaving other vibrant hues far behind. It was a color that usually heralded suffering or trouble, screaming to be acknowledged and dealt with.

All of this simmered above one unfamiliar person, a figure who had joined their table on this playful day. The stranger, who seemed quite friendly, sparked an irresistible temptation in her to reveal to him what she was seeing.

She didn't want to frighten him; she simply wanted to give vent to her emotions because it seemed to her that since it was returning to her, everything she had deeply hidden in the depths of her subconscious must be some kind of sign that something would start to change from now on.

She didn't yet know if it would be for better or worse, and what truly awaited her on this evening.

"It seems to me that there's something off with your body," the stranger said, slightly disoriented.

Looking at her, and after a moment, asked, "What do you mean?"

"I'm not exactly sure, but when I look at you, I sense unease and some kind of problem that you are or will be struggling with."

"What?" (Laughs)

"I don't know, but it seems to me that you should see a doctor," she responded.

The stranger stood up from his seat, seemingly crazed, and she remained alone at the corner of the table where they were sitting.

Great, not only am I sitting alone, but now he thinks I'm a lunatic, she thought proudly, more satisfied with the return of something lost to her.

She savored that feeling for a brief moment, until the rest of her companions returned to the table after likely consuming the entire assortment the bartender had prepared for the evening.

Her friend's gaze was filled with admiration but also concern when she said to her, "You chose a great moment."

"The guy is completely frightened; he has been dealing with a condition called stomia for years."

She froze. She didn't know what she should think at that moment. However, she quickly snapped out of it, remembering that nothing would cause her pain anymore. She tucked that story away in one of her mental drawers and wanted to forget as quickly as possible that the stranger had become her training ground for the return of something she desired.

Hours passed, and the girls were eager to hop from one club to another, with no sign of the party ending anytime soon. On their way from one club to the next, a few of them decided to take a break.

The height of their heels and the thousands of weary steps on the uneven cobblestone street were starting to take a toll on them. They sat on the curb in front of one of the busiest clubs on this side of the city, feeling increasingly drained.

When two of them finally agreed to head home and fetch the rest of the girls who were still having a great time in the club across the street, one of them dashed out, shouting at the top of her slightly softened voice, "Come on! You have to see this!"

Without much hesitation about what could be so worth their attention, they made their way to the club where the rest of the girls had scattered to different areas.

They rushed into the club to find one of them at the bar, sipping her favorite alcoholic drink, whisky with cola, and engrossed in a conversation with someone she deemed interesting in her intoxicated perception.

Another girl was sitting at a table with a group of friends who happened to be at the club at the same time. The rest of them were dancing on the dance floor, or rather, in their current state, it could hardly be called dancing.

Entering the club, she was distracted. On one hand, she wanted to find her friend, but she was already engrossed in a conversation with someone else. On the other hand, she didn't feel particularly inclined to join the others on the dance floor.

One of her friends ran up to her, pulling her by the hand and shouting, "Come on, they're over there, you have to see this!"

They went together to the area referred to as the dance floor, but it was more like a small cage surrounded by mirrors. Several people were dancing in the center, making the view more transparent.

One of their group was dancing with a guy, giving a thumbs-up to signal her choice and how handsome she found him. However, the charm quickly faded when the man genuinely and proudly smiled, revealing prominent imperfections or rather, deficiencies that caught everyone's attention.

No one, except perhaps her, seemed to pay attention to it, as they were too busy enjoying themselves and laughing in the moment that was meant to be here and now.

She had been standing alone for a while as everyone else had returned to the dance floor. She looked around, not seeing any other option for spending these, hopefully, last moments in the club.

She decided to join them on the dance floor. A mirror turned out to be her lifeline, attracting her attention. She approached it to quickly fix her hair and get rid of the nonsense that kept lingering on her head. The last traces of pink color and cynically looking glowing ears found their place at the bottom of her bag.

Standing there for a moment, gazing at her reflection, she saw a sign showing the 'OK' symbol, symbolizing that she looked good. At that moment, she thought, how crude it was for anything to show her anything. After all, she was not a piece of meat that came in search of its dog.

She turned around and froze for a moment. It happened, it struck her. He stood before her, smiling and shining with his beautiful eyes. Little did she know at that moment that she was looking directly into the eyes of the person who would change everything.

She sized him up from head to toe and nodded to herself in a silent agreement. Why not dance with him? After all, she enjoyed dancing, she enjoyed doing all these things before the darkness consumed her.

She took his hands and swayed and danced with him to the rhythm of the music, occasionally turning to face him and gazing deeply into his eyes, which either seemed intoxicated or so beautiful, revealing an enchanting space that captivated her.

They didn't exchange any words that evening, only exchanging glances and gentle smiles. She was carried away by the moment, wanting to initiate a conversation at one point but receiving no response.

She thought that he might be mute, shy, or simply too intoxicated to gather his thoughts. She did something she had never been inclined to do, something she had always mocked upon hearing it in other people's stories.

She gestured to him to input his number on her phone. Several attempts, and still nothing. The number kept being entered incorrectly. Then she asked for his phone to input her number, not really thinking about the consequences or even considering that the next day, this beautiful stranger would remember her at all.

Before she stepped outside, in one final breath of humanity or the percentage swirling in her head, her lips brushed against his cheek as a farewell.

He did exactly the same, but with greater tenderness than she could have imagined. More than the men who likely indulge in weekly clubbing escapades.

She sat outside, trying to recover from the temperature inside the club, accompanied by a friend who lit a cigarette. They ordered a taxi, and like true mothers, they began gathering their children to leave.

As they stood up and headed toward the street leading to the meeting point, someone peculiarly approached her.

"My friend fell in love with you," they said.

She laughed and added, "He's sweet."

They exchanged a few more sentences, realizing that the world is very small and they share a common ground with his friends. Saying a pleasant goodbye, she walked away with her friends, almost instantly forgetting what had transpired that evening.

The journey home was filled with laughter and reminiscing about the silly things they had done. However, it soon became dull and sleepy as the warmth in the taxi lulled them into a drowsy state.

They dispersed to their respective homes and safely retreated into their apartments, permeated with the scent of alcohol and lingering cigarette smoke. She fell asleep, and the next day was meant to be a return to normalcy.

Back to the daily routines that didn't differ much from the past three years of her life when she lived in solitude, with her daughter as her sole companion.

But fate had other plans.

Waking up in the morning, after just a few hours of sleep that exceeded her usual norm, she did what she repeated every morning.

It was part of the therapy she had implemented on her own, encouraged by the doctor who helped her overcome depression and who had been watching over her and her well-being since that day.

Every morning, she wrote a letter, writing to her best friend as if he had never left, with only his phone remaining out of reach. She told him everything, shared various stories and events with him, and then tucked the letter away in a safe place with the others.

This morning, the letter was supposed to summarize the previous evening when she had decided to go somewhere. However, the letter contained a completely different content from what she had been writing before.

I met someone, or at least I think I did because I don't even know their name since they were not very talkative. Oh, you great poet, always finding an answer to every question in your poetic breath, did you mean that when talking about love? What I felt yesterday may seem childish, but I felt your voice then as it said, "You'll see."

As usual, she repeatedly showered him with insults in a tone that only they knew, and only they understood the sarcasm in their remarks. The conclusion of each letter was written in more or less the same manner, requesting his care for her daughter.

The morning passed like any other day; breakfast, playing with her daughter, a walk, and more playtime. She wasn't in the habit of checking her phone because it primarily served as a means of staying connected with her friend and her father, ensuring that everything was fine and there was nothing to worry about.

However, on that day, she felt a strange urge to check her phone, as if she sensed something awaited her. And there it was, a message. A message from an unfamiliar person, sent the previous day, praising her wonderful eyes and a smile that pierced her just at the mere thought of it.

Something strange was happening to her—how could one moment suddenly captivate her mind like this? It couldn't be possible.

She replied as quickly as possible, in the most enigmatic way she could. Glancing at her phone practically every moment, eagerly awaiting a response. Hours passed, and they exchanged messages throughout the entire day.

Unsuspecting, she was increasingly consumed by the need to converse with him, to get to know him. One evening literally changed everything she had worked so hard for over the past few months.

She began each day by reading his messages and ending it with him. Completely engulfed by his charm, secrecy, mystery, and the magnetism that drew her in so intensely that she couldn't resist.

In her letters, she described everything she couldn't explain in words. She depicted the emotions accompanying her and the void she felt during the few-hour breaks in their message exchanges.

She tried to explain to her friend that she couldn't believe what was happening and somehow, this unknown man had found an invisible crack to infiltrate not only her mind but also her heart.

She refrained from calling it love for a long time because how could one fall in love with someone after seeing them for just a few moments? But he gave her more and more of himself, and she opened up, sharing everything with him—her struggles, her dislike for technology, her love for cooking.

She attentively listened to his hobbies, although she rarely understood them, but she respected him for his passion and the way he not only addressed her but also provided her with a sense of immense security and support. He gave her something she should reject, yet she desperately yearned for it.

Weeks passed, and they never ceased to communicate with each other. They accompanied each other in the least significant activities of the day and shared stories about them. They exchanged photographs of things they saw or even of themselves.

However, she kept the biggest secret within herself. She wasn't ashamed of it, but selfishly, she feared that if she revealed the truth about her daughter and her life, the selfless bond they had formed would disappear and never return.

She was being selfish because her emptiness was being filled, and she didn't want to feel worthless again. Understanding the feeling of someone being interested in how her day went and simply their presence making her feel better.

A few weeks later, the connection between them grew so strong that both sides eagerly longed to finally meet. To see each other for the first time and have a face-to-face conversation.

To look into each other's eyes and answer the question of what truly connects them. Where do these constant conversations lead?

She was so excited to finally see him because she knew that the person she only knew from phone conversations was a complete individual, someone extraordinary who had sparked a tiny flame within her.

Someone who deserved to know all the details of her life. She felt like she knew him deeply, that he was the last person on Earth who deserved to know. And above all, her daughter, who was her whole world, should not be hidden as if she didn't exist. It was a sense of pride and happiness that should be shouted to everyone's face.

The day of the meeting arrived. They kept talking to each other until the very last minute before they were to see each other, coming up with ideas and laughing about various things they would do, just to alleviate the nerves they both felt.

After all, they had been talking for weeks, exchanging photos, knowing well what to expect when they met in person, and yet the nerves still permeated both of them. The awkwardness of the greeting and the way they would greet each other remained a mystery.

She arrived at the meeting place first, even though the distance she had to cover was just as great as what he had to overcome to reach her. They had arranged to meet in a city that would never be indifferent to her again, and every street they walked would be a memory of him—his scent, his gaze, his gentle touch.

The rented apartment looked wonderful, clean, and inviting to spend a few days in. They had agreed that due to the long distances they had to travel, they would stay somewhere overnight to have more hours together and get to know each other better.

They deserved it after so many months of talking. She sat and waited, and minutes dragged on like hours, hours like days. A message from him. Before she opened it, dark scenarios raced through her mind. "What are you doing here? He won't show up."

Heavy traffic, I'll be 30 minutes late. It read.

A stone lifted off her heart, meaning that if he still had half an hour left, there was no chance he would stand her up. After all, he had already covered two and a half hours of the journey. However, it didn't diminish the stress she felt.

She hurried down the staircase to the store she had seen while looking for the right apartment number. She bought a bottle of wine, well, she bought two bottles of wine. She rummaged through drawers in search of a corkscrew, and time was now passing at such a pace that while hastily drinking the first glass, the room seemed to spin.

"I'm downstairs."

"I'm coming for you."

Only a few short minutes separated her from seeing him, and in her mind, she was envisioning how she should greet him. Would a simple 'hello' be enough, or should she hug him or kiss his cheek, just like the day she first saw him?

She saw him and walked toward him, hearing only the loud thumping of her heart against her chest. His smile was visible from afar, and his eyes sparkled like the most beautiful stars in the world. He stood there, waiting for her to approach.

The stress had literally paralyzed her the moment he made the first sound to greet her, spreading his arms for an embrace. She stepped back and offered him her hand. (Laughter.)

She couldn't have done anything more ridiculous, but she was so enchanted by him and the fact that he was here, standing in front of her, that she didn't speak for a long time.

Thoughts swirled in her head, memorizing every little detail of him, capturing his scent, his eyes, his smile, and his wonderful full lips. He was so vivid to her and so completely different from the man she thought she remembered from the club.

The photos he sent her didn't capture his beauty at all. It was all too beautiful for her to believe that it was actually happening to her. That the center of his attention was directed solely and exclusively at her.

The great awkwardness that accompanied them caused even the television to disobey, leaving their heartbeats reverberating against the walls, creating an echoing rhythm.

The evening passed, although the wine was starting to fizz in her system, giving her the courage to ask a question.

"Can I hug you?" She mustered the courage to ask.

"Of course."

The question was as awkward as the accompanying answer. Moments of solace filled her as she found herself in his embrace, experiencing a happiness that permeated every fiber of her being, screaming for this moment not to end.

It was a realization of how much she had longed for this and how much she needed this closeness. The boundless trust she bestowed upon him in that moment was a reward for her, a triumph over herself.

The first kiss. Rather, it was a moment in which she pounced on him. But let's go back. The first kiss, filled with magic, passion, and desire. How could one person desire another so intensely without even speaking about it, but instead conveying it through gestures that made them feel it from head to toe?

That moment drove her wild; she desired him so much, falling deeply in love with the feeling as his lips touched hers. His hands held her gently, yet with strength and certainty. The touch of his bare abdomen, his back, the sensation of his breathing skin, and the sound of their racing hearts.

It began; cracks and fissures started appearing on the thick layer of her icy heart, becoming visible in the most prominent places. She was slowly becoming defenseless, capable of feeling and causing the ice to shatter in an instant.

However, the wine she consumed, which left him slightly embarrassed, led her to surrender only to passion, leaving her emotions behind, to be dealt with later. She would analyze them when she could think clearly and when she would be at a greater distance from him than just ten centimeters.

His closeness made her willing to do anything he said without hesitation. Therefore, the best solution for her was to postpone those feelings for later.

She spent the night and morning in his arms, although feeling ashamed of what she had actually done and the fact that since the kiss, she only remembered fragments. Wine had won that night.

However, he was there the next morning, not leaving without a word, tenderly caressing her forehead, saying, "good morning." It was such a piercing feeling that from that day on, she wished it would remain forever.

Without thinking for too long, and wanting to retrieve the memories of the previous night, she started kissing and touching him in the most passionate way she could, the way she knew. They repeated it several times, eventually exhausted.

It was never as awkward between the two of them as it was when they were ready to go for breakfast. In fact, both of them wanted to escape from there as quickly as possible.

While having breakfast, she couldn't stop looking at him. His sight was so wonderful, even when he hungrily bit into his hamburger. She gazed at him, gathering the strength to tell him what she had been delaying for so long, something she shouldn't have been hiding.

Now, she feared his reaction, his response, and his behavior that could hurt her more than the evening before, before the ice began to melt.

"I need to tell you something," she began. "I haven't told you the whole truth from the beginning. I'm not alone."

"Do you have a child?" He asked.

He had read her like an open book.

"Yes, I have a daughter," she replied.

Before he said anything, she immediately told him the story that only her closest ones knew. She didn't go into detail about how her child's father mistreated her or the moments of weakness she had.

She simply said that it was like a bolt from the blue when she least expected it, when she was mourning her friend. That had to be enough for him, or rather, she dropped an atomic bomb on him, something he didn't expect to handle.

His expression changed in the blink of an eye, even though he tried his best not to show how much it affected him. Looking at him, she didn't know if the problem lay in the fact that she was a mother or in the fact that she had hidden it from him from the start.

Continuing the conversation no longer made sense, and he clearly waited to escape from her as quickly as possible. The journey to the train station felt incredibly long, and the silence they bestowed upon each other only confirmed her belief that they were probably seeing each other for the last time.

"It's not about you having a child. It's about me being in a relationship with a girl who also had a child, and it just didn't work out. I can't handle it."

His words echoed in her mind, bouncing from wall to wall, leaving behind only a bitter pain. She got out of the car, politely thanking him for the ride to the train station, kissing him for the last time.

She didn't turn around to see him because her eyes were filled with tears. Why was she crying? They had only seen each other once, excluding their meeting place. They didn't make any promises to each other, yet she felt emptiness and a sense of failure.

She tried to apologize to him on the way back home, wanting to ease the situation, but his response was very decisive. Despite his assurances that it wasn't just her who suffered a defeat because he also lost her in that moment, she felt even worse.

After all, that little being who enters every room cannot be the determining factor of whether someone will love someone else or not. After all, she already knew him and knew that if he gave himself a chance to get to know her daughter, he would love her even more than he loved her.

They remained in contact, but the hours of awkward conversation no longer showed any hope of improving the situation.

Two days of terrible pain, not psychological but physical, made it impossible to forget. The moment she noticed how careless they were and how much they were consumed by boundless passion when leaving the restroom, fear began to make decisions for her. She ran to the phone and wrote a message.

What have you done to me?
What are you talking about?

You played with me and left, and I'll be the one dealing with this! She screamed.

I didn't play with you, you know it's not true. That day, I also lost you, but believe me, it will be better this way.

Something stayed inside me, how could you?

What are you talking about?

You left something behind in me, and that's why I felt so much pain and discomfort all weekend.

What?

You heard me! And now I'll be left dealing with it, once again.

Calm down, I didn't do it on purpose. We got carried away, but now calm down.

It's easy for you to say.

How can I help you? What do you need?

Screw you! She declared.

However, he didn't give up easily; he genuinely seemed very moved by the situation that had unfolded. Okay, they had played around, it didn't work out, and it should end there. She tried to reason with herself in her head, but something like this?

Every day, he asked about her well-being, and she only growled at him in anger. It was anger, but not because of what had happened; rather, because he's not with her now to go through this situation together, to come up with a solution together, and to forget about it together. Parting from each other amicably.

A pill turned out to be their salvation, which her friend somehow managed to get on the last day when they could still mitigate the potential consequences of their memorable night.

The next day was terrible for her—dizziness, vomiting, stomach pain. He remained in constant contact with her, showing her that he truly cares. Even though she kept telling him that he's not concerned about her but only about himself, and the fact that one mistake could ruin his whole life.

That it would tie him to the girl he rejected right from the start, not giving them a chance to see how things could have turned out. Days went by and they were still in touch, a constant battle and exchange of aggressive messages. One afternoon, something changed.

She wrote to him that everything was okay now, that her monthly bloody encounter had just begun, and that she truly apologizes for how she's been toward him lately, but she got scared, and she knows he did too.

She told him that despite how the situation unfolded, he's truly special to her, and she would really like to keep in touch with him. She understands that a romantic relationship might not work out between them because he has his own opinion on that, but friendship is also something they could build.

To her great surprise, he replied that he thought the same way and that he's grateful for everything she wrote to him. They established a friendship.

However, what truly connected them before was becoming more and more apparent to them. And if someone had told them that an unplanned mishap with protection would bring them back together, that they would want to see each other more than ever, each of them would have laughed until they were out of breath. And yet, fate played a trick on them, giving them a chance to get to know each other anew.

Weeks passed, and days began in the same cyclic way. He greeted her with a morning message, where a simple 'good morning' was filled with incredible tenderness and dedication. And she responded in the same manner.

They accompanied each other every day, every hour, every minute. They consumed each other like a drug, wanting more and more. Yearning for each other more with each passing day.

She suggested a meeting to him; she couldn't bear the tension and separation any longer. She needed him like air. They chose the same place, the same city for their meeting, only changing their accommodations to stay closer to the city center.

As was their habit in their short but intensely emotional acquaintance, she arrived first and waited for him. Waiting was nothing like their previous waiting; the nervousness wasn't as apparent anymore, only the longing was stronger than before. After a few hours of solitary waiting, she finally received a call from him:

"I'm here, just looking for a parking spot."

Only minutes separated her from him. A knock at the door, she ran as if on wings and without even giving him a moment to greet her, she threw herself into his arms and began kissing him passionately as intensely as she could.

Once again, she felt what she had longed for—him, his scent, a touch as divine as a brush of an angel's wing, his lips which tenderly returned her kisses, leaving her numb.

Finally, she gave him a moment to at least put his bag down and take a deep breath.

They talked, but she only heard every other word, staring at him like an image, memorizing every inch of him. She wanted this image to stay in her mind, filling her until the next day when they'd get to see each other again.

They fell asleep, embraced in each other's arms like two inseparable beings, connected by the cosmic force of the universe. His breathing quickened, indicating that sleep was completely taking over him.

She, a girl who had struggled with sleep problems for years, was given the chance by fate to spend hours admiring what she had before her eyes, and how wonderful a man lay beside her.

The night was pleasant but too short, and the entire morning they lay together, alternating between talking and making love. She felt so comfortable with him and absorbed every bit of him, not realizing that she was becoming more and more addicted.

The day passed, and she never wanted it to end. They walked around their own city of love like two complete strangers, maintaining a distance between them that didn't resemble what had happened a few hours before.

This excited her even more, as their entire relationship hadn't been obvious from the beginning. It didn't start with an assumption of whether they should refer to themselves as a couple or simply as two individuals spending time together with small diversions.

One thing was certain. Even back then, he was giving her something that could be called a miracle. Each of their meetings was a big unknown; they never knew when it would happen or where it would take place.

Everything began moving faster as if it followed a diabolical, one might say, plan. For years, she hadn't traveled anywhere, and she never really had vacations, especially not with a group of women.

Her former friends quickly agreed to the idea of spending a weekend in a foreign country, where everything that happened would be forgotten immediately. But was it really so?

The days leading up to the trip passed quickly, and they were coming up with newer plans about what they would do and how they intended to spend their time. The rented apartment turned out not to be a luxurious five-star hotel, but rather a run-down place that they didn't mind.

The thought of shopping and partying until morning in places where they wouldn't run into anyone they knew fueled their excitement. Why did they choose that particular place? The answer is trivial—it was the place where he, her dream prince from a fairytale, had lived.

The day of their arrival proved quite exhausting due to the number of stops and the distances they had to cover, but they didn't give in to their fatigue. In the blink of an eye, they changed into their evening outfits while sipping alcoholic drinks to get into a preliminary good mood. However, she had all her energy and thoughts focused in one direction. She couldn't wait anymore.

When she would finally see him. She dreamed of the moment when she would throw herself into his arms and confess how much she missed him, almost not believing it herself.

The cobblestone road was bumpy, and it wasn't easy for them to traverse every meter in the shoes they had chosen for the evening. Comfort didn't matter then; after all, they had gone somewhere together and intended to do what constrained them on a daily basis.

Walking down a narrow alley that resembled anything but a romantic pathway, only a crowded, bustling, alcohol-infused, laughter-filled place where everyone resets after a week of hard work.

And there he was, in front of her eyes, standing in his favorite jacket, its color accentuating the shade of his complexion. His hair was perfectly styled, as he was accustomed to appearing in public places.

He stood there, waiting for her, the girl who was losing her breath with every passing second as they got closer. The sparkle in his eyes upon seeing her could illuminate any room in the world. The smile he bestowed upon her pierced and electrified every inch of her body.

Despite the noise, shouts, and laughter, they couldn't dispel the awkward atmosphere that surrounded them. Even though they had both been waiting for this moment, they weren't quite sure how to behave in the presence of others and how to respond to the questions asked by those around them.

It seemed like an obvious thing, but also uncertain. They all continued talking for a while, standing outside and exchanging travel stories while getting to know each other.

A friend who was accompanying them that evening took complete initiative in the conversation and in looking after her companions, leaving them alone outside, so they could enjoy each other's company for a while.

Nestled in him, she couldn't stop herself from being close to him for even a single moment, inhaling his scent and whispering in his ear. The euphoria she felt at that time made her feel like she was in a drug-induced haze.

She got lost gazing into his eyes; did she already know then that he was the one? That he did something that no one had managed in her life before? Did he awaken her feelings? Or at least make her consider that these feelings might apply to her?

Yes, he ignited a small spark within her, which on that day started smoldering and slowly transformed into a tiny flame. Did she do the same to him? Yes. What connected them was odd through and through, but they both wanted more. What changed since that moment? Literally everything changed.

Close your eyes and imagine that this girl, about whom you've learned so much, once had wings. Beautiful, long, white angelic wings, where each feather perfectly aligned with the next, shining and dazzling everyone around when they unfurled and prepared for flight.

Wings that were abruptly severed so long ago, leaving scars and indentations on her back, reminders of what happiness used to be, something she would never experience again.

The wounds burned and itched, constantly reminding her of their existence in moments when she was so close to forgetting about them. That's what the existence of a fallen angel looked like, spiraling into dust.

Nevertheless, people often say that the true strength of the world lies in being like a phoenix, a creature that, in its grace and dignity, despite the opinions of others, looking them straight in the eye, can combust and turn to ash.

And from that ash, rise even more splendidly in all its magnificence than anyone had the chance to see before. Did she feel that way back then? No. She felt a sensation as if the burning in her back had subsided. She felt a gentle pounding, billions of tiny needles striking her scars.

"I love you," unexpected yet incredibly tender confession was like a golden key emanating from his lips, going straight to the lock attached to her body, ready to twist the mechanism and nourish thirsty sprouts so they could grow.

"Give me water, and thirst will cease. Give me food, and hunger will cease. Give me love, and I will show you wings that will guide us farther." That's how she felt, as if the wings were visible on her body again, their shadow becoming more prominent with each subsequent declaration of love.

"I love you," he repeated with great embarrassment once again, probably waiting for her reaction or reciprocation of those words.

"It's imprudent and too early, not so quickly, it can't happen so fast." The words tumbled out of her mouth, adding, "Damn it, I've fallen for you," kissing him, not wanting to hear anything else for the moment.

They entered inside, taking their seats at a table with the rest of the company, placing themselves apart as if what had just happened had never occurred.

The evening had no end, and they gazed at each other, not needing to catch their breath. They didn't need it. From that moment on, they only needed each other.

They changed venues; the night was still young, and the amount of alcohol flowing through the girls' veins amplified the craving for dancing and the euphoria of fun.

The music pulsated, filling the entire two-level space, and the energy of the people in the place encouraged everyone to make the most of their time in the most effective way possible. They danced, they drank, and they simply lived.

Did she already know then, despite the confession of love, that she was spending the night with the love of her life? No. In her dictionary, the concept of a love that would last forever didn't exist. But remember, every dictionary can be reprinted.

Darkness

"Where are you?"

"I'm here."

"Where are you really?"

Have you ever felt like you're there, but it's as if you're not really there at all? She felt, she loved/fought. Present in body, absent in thoughts. Smiling on the outside, stone inside.

Everyone dwelling in darkness floats in a black mass, feeling absolute calm and bliss. No fear of suffering, no fear of new suffering. They hunker down there, seeking refuge, shielded like a protective barrier. And whatever happens gets absorbed there, leaving no memories or marks behind.

That's how it was supposed to be, that's how she made it, not realizing that often in the darkness, when we lower our gaze, something unplanned happens. You linger in it so long that you don't notice the metaphorical flicker of light passing by.

At first, it's just a flash, and it appears very rarely. You're capable of ignoring it, turning your head away, and waiting for it to fade. But that light doesn't give up; it reappears again and again, and you watch it with curiosity and a hint of reservation. This foreign phenomenon piques your interest, until the game begins. The game called life and death.

They spent their days' together, writing and calling, their conversations endless as they delved into the deepest corners of their souls. With each passing day, they learned more and more about each other, unable to function without one another.

She couldn't. She waged a battle against herself, but all too often, more often than she should, she let her guard down and surrendered to everything.

She felt longing, but not the kind that was so familiar to her, not the kind that might have been a direct ticket to the darkness. This was something unfamiliar, not filled with suffering, pain, and sorrow.

Longing, beautiful in its light, propelling her toward happiness. Longing for the scent, the touch, the gesture, the gaze.

The planned meetings, yes, they were planned, as their relationship didn't entertain spontaneity, were short but rare. Yet, they could extract the essence that flowed from them, staying within their comfort zone.

She wanted more, that was clear, and he wanted even more. She couldn't give him that, couldn't see him more often despite her heart's cries. She shielded herself from happiness, often winning that battle.

The back of her mind was aware that if she allowed for more, unresolved issues, hidden deep in the drawers of her being, would resurface and she would have to face them. It was simply selfishly convenient for her to leave everything as it was, waiting for a miracle that would magically solve everything for her. But was that really the point?

It seems to me that she lived more with the conviction of whether this feeling that had fallen upon her was real and if it would stay with her as one drawer after another began to open.

Would they endure, and are his assurances that he would wait as long as she needed truly genuine? Is he fully aware of the situation that awaits them? She analyzed every word of his, throwing it at him at the slightest opportunity, wanting to make sure he hadn't changed his stance.

He had been saying it for so long that she believed him. Supposedly, faith is a trait that's deceptive, much like hope; it's not a tangible entity you can sit down with and weigh the pros and cons.

They talked for so many months, they were there for each other in the toughest moments, they saw each other's tears. They laid themselves bare, leaving no room for unspoken pasts; they knew everything about each other.

They knew each other's falls and the stories etched in their souls. About memories from their youth, never spoken aloud. About things one can only delve into and speak about to the person they trust unconditionally, the one who still looks at you with eyes filled with love even after you finish your last sentence.

They created their own world, one meant just for them, living in it, revealing themselves and being themselves. She showed him only the person she was now, she never mustered the courage to show him who she used to be, and he probably would have liked that version even more.

And even though the past often crept in during their meetings, she laughed and gave everything she could. She woke up from her lethargy and returned to the stone-like state she once was. She teetered on the edge.

All the romantic moments they shared, she recorded in her mind, waiting for her own moments of conversation with herself, translating them onto paper as she was accustomed to.

Usually ending each of her written outpourings of thoughts in the same schematic way, "I won't forget, I won't allow happiness to let me forget, I'm sorry I allowed myself to."

And despite wanting to, she couldn't move forward, constantly retreating. Three critical steps forward and a whole mass backward. A vicious cycle from which she couldn't escape, or at least that's how it seemed to her.

She couldn't, after everything that had happened, not after the loss and suffering she had experienced. She couldn't embrace happiness, knowing that she had taken life away.

All the destructive decisions she made led her even deeper into the darkness. Insomnia plagued her even more than the years that had become the norm in this state. She loved him, trying to give him the most precious thing, worth more than all beings in the world.

In doing so, she fell into the same machine of events that must have had their consequences later on. However, in her wildest nightmares, she didn't expect that she would be hit by the ricochet of what she desired and what had held her firmly, giving her strength when she first tried to do everything right.

When she made the decision that truly propelled her, that despite everything he knew about her, he would stay with her and guide her through the turbulent waves of the ocean, so that at the end of the journey, they could sit together, wrapped in each other, feeling that it was all worth it. And now, they could start a new chapter of their own story without any obstacles.

Hope, an intangible void that propels you into action. It exploits the remnants of your strength and pushes you to do things, make decisions, all while awaiting to receive something.

A reward? Glory? Nothing at all. Hope gives nothing, and it has long been attributed as a co-dependent factor of human existence. Hope is the sustenance of fools.

What's tangible, and what can truly show you the effect of your efforts? I believe only a miracle. Miracles happen, they say, when you hardly believe in them. Although, even with that belief, it varies for each individual. Nevertheless, the word hope should never be met with approval from people.

Hope drains you, you live it in a loop, and hope dies last. Nonsense. You die because that hope has cleansed you of everything. You die, knowing that even your hope wasn't able to hold you to life.

Remember, there is no hope. Because it reaps more powerful harvests than death.

There were days when she couldn't even handle her love for him, her feelings becoming increasingly incomprehensible to herself. She yearned for him deeply, loved him, and counted down the days until they could meet again.

Their encounters, the greetings full of passion, with a sparkle in their eyes, made both of them aware that they belonged completely to each other. She vividly remembers one of their meetings in particular, after a long separation when they could finally see each other.

The day was beautifully sunny, and he was already waiting for her in their city to take her to his place for a few days. The moment their lips met gave her the sensation as if they had never parted before, as if there had never been any distance between them, as if every second of their lives had been filled with each other.

They got into the car and, like two people in love more than anything in the world, they set off. The music played from the speakers, and she lost herself in singing, even though she knew she wasn't really good at it.

His love and happiness of being together in that moment were always conveyed in the same tender way, the most beautiful way a beloved woman can imagine. Wasn't it every woman's dream for a man to sometimes express his love more with actions than words?

That's exactly how he was. Tender kisses on her hand, holding her hand tightly during the nearly three-hour journey—these were more than just physical closeness. It was a prelude to the moments when they would be able to truly connect, when both of them, nestled in each other's arms, would rediscover one another.

His taste would permeate every inch of her body. She would nibble on the tips of his ears, making him want more and more with every passing minute. That's who they were, deeply in love, writing their own story.

A story that, as you will see for yourselves, they couldn't bring to an end. It's an incredibly winding tale, but one that lasts eternally.

And suddenly, everything falls to the floor; they can't wait any longer. His strength, along with his incredible tenderness, pressed her against the wall of his foyer, and in passionate embraces, he penetrated her body more deeply.

Two breaths merging into one, synchronized heartbeats producing the sound of their accelerated pulses. They longed to become one, now disregarding everything else. It consumed them like an abyss, an eternal insatiability. Romantic, yet intensely filled with brutality, their passionate kisses fueled ever-increasing arousal.

The struggle to prolong this moment, to make it last as long as possible, often ended in failure for one of them, unable to hold on any longer. The haste to remove clothes, the touch of bodies no longer shielded by anything that could hide their naturalness, until the moment when one tasted the other.

The romance of these moments was never one of silence; it was a constant stream of words, the sounds of their breath escaping them. Declarations of love, attraction, and immense excitement echoed off the walls, which memorized every moment of their passions.

His admiration for her body always evoked a sense of shyness within her, yet internally, it worked on her like a drug. Swift accelerations, slowdowns, a constant hunger. Always craving more.

He knew every inch of her body, understood her needs, likes, and what he could allow himself. He knew her better than she could ever imagine. His touch was unlike anything she had experienced before, he loved her like no one else in the world, and he desired her with an intensity only he could muster.

Every morning, he prepared breakfast for her. The scent of fresh bread and their shared conversations were a magical start to each day. The gentle brush of his lips against her arm sent shivers down her spine at the mere thought of it. The prospect of these days spent together was meant to be endless.

Breakfast in the most romantic atmosphere led to more romantic moments, and their days were never routine. Even though from an outsider's perspective, they might not resemble a carousel or a stormy sea, they were anything but ordinary days filled with extraordinary moments.

While shopping at the supermarket, they picked out products that best suited their afternoon plan, a plan that fulfilled both of their dreams in its uniqueness. A simple trip to the lake, an ordinary picnic, yet so extraordinary.

They had never done this together before, never spent time in this way, never truly enjoyed nature, and never had the chance to be themselves in their daily activities and passions. So, what was his passion? Who was this extraordinary person?

He loved nature, and nature loved him—they were united, 1:1. He could talk for hours about what fascinated him and what he truly did.

He showed her the essence of fishing, which previously in her eyes was nothing more than a boring activity that men engaged in, sitting on the shore with a fishing rod, gazing at the water for hours, which could be as enchanting and enigmatic as it was impenetrable for many hours.

He was different. He told her that the key was in the approach, in the preparation, in what you feed the waters with to get what you desire in return. He was passionate about making the catch as large as possible, always treating it with care, and releasing it gently afterward.

She was fascinated by how he did it, how he spoke about it, and how much heart he put into it. To her surprise, it began to captivate her even more than she could have imagined.

On that day, they had a picnic by one of his favorite lakes. They sunk their fishing lines into the water together, and then lay on a blanket, gazing at the sky, daydreaming, cuddling, and capturing every moment they spent together.

Every twitch of the fishing rod, every small noise, was a result of her exuberant scream in the rush of emotions as they successfully caught something together. On that day, every alarm was false, and her behavior melted him to the core.

This day could last forever. He spoke words to her that no one had uttered before, and through her actions, she did something he had never had the chance to do with anyone else. It was their shared first time. No other woman had been able to participate in what she could be on that day.

They knew their bodies by heart, every millimeter was their domain. That's why he boldly jumped into the water naked, swimming freely. In return, her gaze devoured him with patterns, conveying that he was the most beautiful and energetic person to her.

Often unable to control her own excitement at the sight of him, she bit her lip with her teeth. He knew all too well the effect he had on her, so he pushed himself to the heights of his masculinity, not wanting to make that moment any easier for her.

The day unfolded in the best way, and they returned home, full of love and contentment, ready to relive that moment the next day. When she was close to him, she knew she could spend the rest of her life like that. Nothing more was needed for her happiness—just him, that moment, and their little daughter who would fill the gap.

Every evening, as she lay down next to him, she would hug him tightly and kiss him with all her might, closing her eyes and dreaming not only of a shared future but also of him—of who he was and the immense, liberated happiness she was lucky to have.

When she knew that after the afternoon paradise with him, the moment of returning to reality, to her normal life, was imminent, tears would well up in her eyes.

She could never hold back the bitterness that overwhelmed her then, but he, in the strength of his love, offered her more and more, wanting to spend more time with her. He would drive her back, wanting to prolong the moment of parting as much as possible.

And if anyone ever asked her who he was to her, more than just love and a partner, without hesitation, she would say he was her hero. He was her fairy tale prince who came to rescue her, who arrived to turn the wheel of fortune and show her the world—a world without fear, pain, filled with the most beautiful colors of life.

Now I'm thinking about how her world would look, her world with him, if her courage were the same as it was later? How many shared stories would they have already written and how many beautiful moments experienced together. When neither of them felt the taste of bitterness, disappointment sadness, and all that fucking loss.

Once she would have said about them that they were like a prince and princess from a fairy tale. Floating on a pink cloud made of cotton candy. Now knowing their story, I know one thing.

It was and still is true love, which few have the chance to even taste to a small extent. Their love required work, falls, returns, loss, and most importantly, understanding. How did they do? Time will tell.

Because time heals wounds. Although I believe that time only allows us to look at those wounds differently. We remember, but it hurts less. Doesn't burn. Doesn't give discomfort. It just is and reminds us of itself with its itching.

One body nestled in another body, feeling the morning breeze, which crept in through the window opening. Goosebumps conveying their human sensations, heightened by the sense of closeness to him.

A gentle brush of a kiss on the arm, the one she came to love most deeply, the loud thumping of hearts escaping their chests, waiting only for that one morning gesture. A murmur and a strong embrace as she nestled into his arms, a sign of greeting for another beautiful shared day.

Was there anything more beautiful for them in that moment than the time they gazed deeply into each other's eyes, when their bodies merged? Hearts beat in a shared rhythm, and every particle existing in the universe fell asleep peacefully, feeling their irreplaceable tranquility?

That's what they were like. Full of passion, concealed behind the veil of the darkness of secrecy, running toward the light. Knowing that whatever happens, people like them cannot be forgotten. It won't work out separately for them, and together, it will be tough. They knew, even then.

Goodbyes were never easy, and they themselves could never quite get used to them. Tears, longing, even though they were still together, still touching, still unified. Every time repeating, this is not a farewell. This is not a farewell.

Trying to see it through her eyes, her feelings, now it makes more sense. There was always a fear in them, always accompanied them at every meeting. The fear that each subsequent one could be the last? Why?

They loved each other so much, didn't they? Could you love too much? Why? Maybe when I find the answer to this question? Even they themselves didn't know.

Fight

The moment had come when it happened, something she had tried so hard to avoid. No one would understand the fear she felt, and how much effort it took to make that decision. She wanted to check if she could still live, she wanted to live with him, she felt it, she desired it.

She ignited a war, leaving behind scattered victims, walking past them indifferently. But her heart beat, even though it shouldn't. She didn't even know in which exact moment she had made the decision and said, "ENOUGH!" But she knew for sure what was driving her. Him.

She realized that the recent events had left such a strong mark on her that the fossils had slowly started to crumble, although she wasn't yet aware of how much.

Let's start from the beginning, with what she truly had to fight. Her battle had been going on for the last years of her life. However, to win the ultimate war, she had to deal with something else, and that filled her with unimaginable fear, even though fear and apprehension were not foreign to her. The demons that danced at night were now invited into the daylight to reveal their beauty.

A story written by the mouths of others. Familiar?

Her whole life, she aimed to be perfect for others, sacrificing herself and wanting to bring satisfaction from herself. She wanted so much to make the world better, and so much for everyone to be proud of her.

Despite making wrong decisions throughout her life, she still wanted to bring pride in the end. Often, it was about small things, but they were also issues that burdened the entire family.

One of them was undoubtedly the opinions of other people. Her family, though quite well-known in the town she came from, never flaunted their lives, yet everyone knew everything.

Whether it was because of her mom's recognizability or other reasons, they were certainly on the society's radar, or so it seemed. Her mother, who held a position in a state institution recognized throughout the city, always dealt with the stigma left on her by her recognized face.

Being perfect and impeccable had always been the yardstick of others' opinions for her. Her entire professional and private life was measured against comments about her exemplary family.

Her loving husband was put on a pedestal, and her daughters were considered role models. She raised them in a manner that many would consider quite strict, but in her conviction, she believed that only this way would they achieve independence and self-sufficiency.

She repeated to them every day that their choices would leave a thick mark on their later lives, and they could never allow themselves to be dependent on someone else.

Seemingly trivial, yet on the other hand quite improbable, because even though she instilled this deeply in them, she never truly allowed them to make their own decisions a hundred percent, leaving a psychological imprint on them.

What mattered to her more than her children's happiness? I don't know, she probably would have said that people's opinions did matter at some point, and then it changed in an instant. But I'll get to that calmly.

One of her daughters had always filled her with pride— good choices, good upbringing, a life path laid out in the same schematic way as probably half of society. Coming home on time, asking for permission for various desires, and later on, love.

A storybook relationship, culminating in marriage and starting a family. Admiring the picture, you wouldn't see any hesitation in her brush strokes as she applied the next color. The pursuit of perfection, truly worthy of a novel about a perfectly created home hearth.

The second daughter, raised in the same family, in the same tried-and-tested way, yet with results completely different from the first version. She lived in her own world as far back as she could remember, taking on the most unrealistic roles during play in her childhood.

She never wanted to measure up to any standards. She seemed to have always known what she truly wanted in life and what she could afford. Her childhood dreams of the future were radically different from those of her peers.

She never saw the shimmering beauty in remaining a princess, probably because from a young age, she knew it was all nonsense. The abstraction of defining herself intrigued her, conveying the message that she wasn't an ordinary child.

Friends came and went, not staying long in her life. Even back then, she didn't keep people around who were insignificant and didn't contribute anything to her life.

She chose her company cautiously, without analyzing each case individually; people simply stayed with her who could see the beauty within her ugliness of character. And she knew how to show them that beauty.

With each passing year, as she increasingly entered adulthood, the profession she was giving her mother began to feel more like a metaphorical expression, suggesting that with each new escapade, she was taking ten years off her mother's life.

Her childhood had already become an open book, where her father's struggle to regain his mobility is well-known.

Everything else that happened in her teenage life was probably a consequence not only of youthful rebellion but also a sort of reaction to random events. Rebellion served as a turning point for her, explaining both her behavior and the behaviors she directed toward her surroundings.

Poor choices shaped and refined her character in a way that many will never have the opportunity to experience. One of the first refinements etched into her soul is probably the moment when she decided to try adulthood for herself and live without the belief that she would owe anyone anything.

A pivotal departure that changed her previous place of residence, a foreign world, unfamiliar people, and only a handful of unchanging friends. A new adventure that was meant to be a fresh start to her adulthood.

A country she knew quite a bit about, enough to step into it. Despite her mother's objections and thanks to her father's support, she packed her bags and embarked on a two-year journey, disregarding her mother's opinions and disappointment that she was taking a break while chores and wells would wait, she would say with a big smile on her face.

The first few months went by quickly, not bringing any significant changes to her life. Only new friends, a new job, a new place to live, and an overwhelming sense of boredom. The idea of a carefree life without supervision dissolved in the air.

Routine made itself known, offering only a small outlet when the person she was involved with at the time provided occasional entertaining distractions, pulling her out of the safe world of independence.

She had a youthful infatuation, or rather attempts to step into adulthood with a guy who was never her idea of an ideal life partner. Declarations of love never crossed her mind, as she simply didn't believe in that as a child.

They spent time together in the most normal way, with one small exception. Outbursts of aggression always ended the same way, and she took on a new persona; a punching bag. And although she never remained indebted, it became increasingly exhausting for her.

Concealing everything that marked her body in some strange way didn't emotionally scar her. She found herself in it because she probably explained it to herself as something normal.

After all, she wasn't a passive victim; she wasn't blameless, so she shouldn't have any grievances either. It was all temporary; she could have said enough and ended the situation, just returning home as if nothing had happened. However, her pride wouldn't allow it.

She couldn't admit her mistake to her mother; she couldn't reveal how right she was, how everything her mother had said was bearing fruit.

Everything changed one evening. She was sleeping in her upstairs bedroom, reached by steep wooden stairs. She was awakened by noise and incoherent muttering coming from someone.

That night, she was probably alone in the house, as the other occupants were working the evening shift. She wasn't easily frightened, but ever since she arrived in that house, it had always stirred a kind of fear in her—more than usual, especially when she was alone in it in the evenings.

Whether it was due to the location or simply her uneasiness about a country that wasn't hers, I don't know, but it's certain that nights were not the easiest for her. The noise and muttering, familiar muttering.

She got up and walked over to the bedroom door, ready to lock it when the moment came, so she wouldn't have to listen to a drunk and goodness-knows-what-else person with their existential grievances throughout the night.

He didn't knock on the door. he was strangely calm, and unsuspecting, she went outside. They looked at each other for a moment, and then seeing his state, she decided to go downstairs for water.

Did her movement trigger the situation turning against her, or was it just the calm before the storm? He grabbed her and pulled, shouting, and while she struggled against him, she also pushed him away, shouting for him to just back off.

She couldn't let go, and she never wanted to calm him down; she was perhaps deriving a peculiar form of entertainment from this world she had been living in for a while.

The situation momentarily calmed down when the usual words were spoken, telling him to go to sleep because he would regret it again. But this time, it didn't work for long, and with all his strength, he pushed her toward the stairs.

Three broken ribs, a twisted wrist, the prospect of being housebound for a month. Fantastic. Now the euphoria flowed through her vision, and she could sense her family's distress reaching its zenith.

Time was working against her, and the youthful antics, which she probably didn't understand, had to come to an end. Her best friend didn't hesitate for a moment when he heard about the incident, especially its consequences. Alongside her beloved father, they were at the scene the same day, taking her home.

They didn't judge, they didn't ask. They decided to handle it themselves. Put an end to the rebellion she harbored. Did they understand the situation and what was driving her? Probably.

Was it an attempt to draw attention to herself? I don't know but one thing is certain; the no-approach order was like a sentence.

"This has to end," her friend's voice resonated.

"It's not healthy. She won't understand. You need to forgive her and accept her for who she is."

"I still feel inferior to her."

The same conversations about her mother persisted, even in those moments when her mother seemed to not comprehend her. Yet she was so mistaken; her mother was supporting her, she just couldn't display it.

Something was obscuring her clear understanding of the situation. She was suffering greatly, and all she could do was confess why she never told her mother what she truly felt.

It didn't help either of them. They continued to live within their peculiar relationship.

Years went by, and the voice in her head kept echoing the words filled with enough shame that they couldn't leave her. She changed everything. She returned to her studies, learned, and gained progressively better professional experiences. She always knew she could achieve more if only she allowed herself.

She increasingly felt the approval and pride her family showed her. There was something to boast about—studies completed with top results, a job that the younger generation could only dream of, climbing the career ladder to reach where she was at the age of just twenty-two.

She already had everything people worked their whole lives for; complete independence was hers. Material possessions never gave her complete satisfaction, yet she had it all without exerting herself too much.

Apartment, car, job, trips—everything belonged to her, and yet it didn't really belong to her. It was all for show; her mother had to be proud when talking about her to everyone. This was the awaited moment, when with pride she presented her daughter in the spotlight of admiration after so many years.

When every member of that society marveled at her, expressing words of praise, interspersed with requests for tips on child rearing. What did she think about this? It was a grand and damn vain pursuit. She wasn't vain herself, she just assigned vanity to certain aspects of her life for those who so desperately needed it.

She lived in this world, surrounded by friends who understood the situation perfectly, offering her support and allowing moments of forgetfulness. They did things that people her age should do.

They allowed her to forget that around them, she didn't need to wear the mask of an adult. They let her be herself. They provided relief from the daily pressure of her family's aspirations. But was what she had achieved and reached the greatest shot fired in her direction? No.

The situation intensified when routine medical tests revealed the truth about her future. It wasn't a death sentence, she probably understands that now. But as someone stripped of the need for personal gratification and dominated by the need to satisfy others, she took it as another piece in the puzzle of a pyramid reaching its goal.

The chances were slim, and she, being in a relationship, tried. The results were fruitless for months. It's tough, it has to be but the pressure on her was immense. The family's expectations created a fog in her mind, making it hard for her to think clearly.

She started desiring the outcome just as much as anyone would, until that memorable day when her relationship was simply marked by another person. She let go, and she put all attempts on hold for an indefinite future.

Accident, death, pregnancy, childbirth, pain. It wasn't supposed to be like this. Could anything else be placed in her path? Of course, a wedding. Did she believe that everyone had changed upon seeing what she was struggling with? Of course. Did she think that no one would use this against her? Of course.

Was she foolish to think she was making the best decisions? Of course. Did she want to turn back? Of course. Could she have turned back? Of course. Did she dare to turn back? No. Not then and not for a long time.

Are the words 'nobody will know it's your child, neighbors will think you're just taking care of it', 'a child without marriage', 'nobody saw you pregnant, we'll explain it away', familiar to anyone? The same nonsense repeated over and over again.

Hearing those words over and over again, her already burdened psyche followed them, once again willing to please everyone around her without thinking about herself. The phrases etched into her mind—'forget about yourself, her happiness matters now, she must have a complete family'—were embedded like a steel sword.

The wedding day, only three months after giving birth when everything still felt so foreign, when physical pain persisted, when her body was subjected to torture, when despite refusal and tears, she was constantly exploited, she had to put on a white dress.

Tears streamed down her cheeks throughout that day, they were not tears of happiness. they were cries for help, for rescue that never came.

Continuous makeup touch-ups were in vain as tears flowed like a raging stream, refusing to stop. The event that gathered a sizable audience had to go on. Although unhappy on the day she had heard about her whole life, a day that was supposed to be like a fairytale, turning beauty into gold, she persisted in sorrow and regret, wearing only a smile that concealed the enormity of her mistake.

And even though she hoped that someone would give her a signal to dramatically escape, deep down, she knew that the unavoidable must come true. The hours dragged on infinitely, and she felt like she was in a circus, where in the arena of her life, she had to put on a performance worthy of an Oscar-winning role.

In a moment, or rather during her months-long psychological weakness, she was exploited by someone who should have been her anchor of happiness. The blow struck when she was at her weakest, when her emotions were being torn apart. Unable to make conscious decisions, she was coerced and manipulated.

The state she found herself in couldn't be called a marriage, and looking at it objectively years later, one might even venture to say that if she could muster the strength within herself, she could attempt to nullify this state.

Perhaps someday that will happen. But for now, she lived as if half-dead. Control and possessiveness took a toll on her when she, strong enough to return to her professional life, decided to step out of the confines of her home. Unaware of how much burden she would take upon herself.

Every journey she took to work or anywhere was meticulously monitored and subjected to analysis, and each day ended the same way—attempting to explain that she was at work, despite car records showing frequent movement.

Despite her sanctuary, where she lived, nothing was private for her during that time. Stripped of the remnants of her own dignity, she persisted and lived as strong as she could for her daughter, turning everything into routine.

The walls witnessed more, yet remained unable to speak. Countless nights of tears, millions of plans swirling in her mind—every morning, she had to bury them deep again so that without a spark of consciousness drifting away, she could survive or function through another day.

She confronted this every day for the next two years of her life, seeking help from individuals who, to varying degrees, had led her down this path themselves. Why did she do this?

Illusions probably still clung to her, that perhaps they were aware of what was happening behind closed doors and would help her endure. They would simply help. However, none of this was to be fulfilled in the immediate future.

"People need to connect."

"Nowhere is perfect."

"He's too good for you anyway, you won't find anyone better."

"Who would want you after all this, a single mother."

She just believed in it. She chose the easiest solution for herself—she simply endured. And despite having said enough and wanting to leave, she remained in a legally unresolved situation for a long time.

After all, she didn't know that something was coming, and the thought of not stirring up trouble made her accept things as they were.

She was alone with her daughter, feeling better, capable of more, and satisfying others with their own imagined idea that maybe someday things would get better, that it was a transitional period. She knew it wouldn't, but selfishly, she allowed people to think that way.

Her own battle continued, uncertain of who the victor would be. because only when the support of her own small army arrived, she decided that she would be the victor. She would win and bask in the glory.

Who was her own army? Him, the only person in the world who showed her fear in different shades, a fear that, despite paralyzing her, was bearable. It was him, even with the distance between them, who reached her core, unconsciously for a long time, stoking her will to fight. She weakened, and he appeared, her shield behind which she took cover.

The battle wasn't evenly matched; emotions against imaginations intertwined with reality were difficult to overcome. Despite assurances of boundless love, support, devotion, and expectations, it took just a moment and a small emotional manipulation involving her child to make her surrender her weapons and start everything anew.

This battle went on for too long, as its insidious grip sapped her strength month after month, not only hers but also her army's.

For too long, she had sought to please everyone else living her life, forgetting what it's like to live by her own principles and beliefs. Unaware at the time, she broke her own heart once again.

Her love's strength wasn't enough. Not then. They won.

Slide Five

"You're the love of my life," he used to say.

She closes her eyes and hears those words. His words always calmed her, her emotions would soar, and he held the key to every one of her reactions. It was always him who made everything look different than her eyes saw it.

The support and words of encouragement that came from his mouth would soothe a new wound every time she was hurt. He loved her despite everything, despite all the crap that surrounded her, that surrounded their love.

Did he see something in her that others didn't? I don't know. Was she worth waiting for? I don't know. One thing I know for sure is that their love was worth it all.

With darkness, it's as if it takes away something we only momentarily release from our sight. She was so grateful to him for just being there, for his love and understanding, that she lost sight of the moment when her selfish absorption in her own life's mess spilled onto him.

It surrounded him from all sides, pierced him through, and every time he fought and stood with her. She saw it too often, saw that darkness overpowering the best she had, she understood, but she also wanted to be so blind.

Her demons were stronger than ever, subduing her with agonizing kisses, and too often, she didn't know how to resist them. Was it due to helplessness or fear? Probably it stemmed from a lack of inner strength to leave her comfort zone. Boundless self-sacrifice in the name of love.

He forgave her too many times, so that she could, in time, see everything that her own war truly carried. She led the battle, forgetting that karma also decides to collect its toll.

Emotions surged within her, and she repeatedly chastised herself, pushing away the happiness she needed, stepping into the fight to be with that happiness. She didn't quite understand its essence. Too much from unresolved matters had lost her once again.

Now, she was inflicting harm herself. She had become so soaked in her own self-mutilation and deprivation of inner joy that she started taking it away from others. With small bites, she stole happiness and strength from the one who had been her salvation.

She blocked everything that could have been meant for them. She was destroying him. Slowly, she killed everything he had offered her, consumed by selfish thoughts only about herself.

She wanted to think about him, it seemed to her that she was thinking about him all the time, but reality presented itself differently. She knew how much strength she should find within herself to fight for him, but she was so afraid.

What did she expect from him? Surely, she expected too much from him. He gave her everything, yet it was never enough for her. Did she subconsciously want him to take her by the hand and guide her through it all like a child?

She was too lost to think clearly. She was definitely too consumed by the belief that he would stay forever. Reality was shaping the small steps of changes that were coming into their lives.

The end of summer, yet the warm gusts of wind didn't allow one to forget about it. The sun, in its most splendid form, bestowed its rays upon everyone thirsty for happiness. However, she was losing herself in the understanding of that concept, taking crumbs from anyone who mattered to her more than she could imagine.

It's obvious that the greatest happiness in her life was her little being, but deep down, she had always known, ever since he appeared, that her complete happiness had his image. The two of them stood on the podium of her life.

It was for them that she loved the strongest in the world, it was for them that she would give her life, they were the ones who brought life back to her, even though she realized it too late.

A week like any other, routine interspersed with anticipation of his arrival. She counted down the days until they would meet, rejoiced, and planned every smallest detail that should be perfect during that time.

Four days, with which she was to be gifted, days spent only with him. Days they were going to spend for the first time in her oasis. Her haven was finally going to be graced with the beauty of his presence, filling every element of her familiar places.

She desired it so much that the time separating her from it was filled, down to the second, with devising and planning. Her dreams began to take on colors.

Shades of gray and black, the scent of the darkness's odor did as it pleased with her, winning whenever it desired. She couldn't fight it, always giving it what it wanted, feeding it.

They were only minutes apart, just a moment and they were going to unite with their boundless love. Waiting for him practically turned her world upside down, as she repeatedly cleaned and arranged things to make him feel as comfortable as possible.

She cooked and tended to dishes, hoping to touch his heart even deeper, as if that were possible. Nervous and anxious, she ran around from morning, trying to control her own sense of fear.

She knew him so well, loved him so deeply, and yet the fear she felt permeated her completely. What was she afraid of? After all, it was him—the man who saw in her what she couldn't understand for so long, the man for whom only she mattered, her well-being, her happiness, her smile.

The man who, with a small gesture and a look, had given himself to her more than anyone else in the world. It took just a moment, a moment when she momentarily looked back, a moment that ruined all the recent days of preparation, days of longing, days when she was supposed to show him how much she loved him.

Distance had never mattered, as they said home is where your heart is. Her home was in his heart, every single beat was another breath of life. Words about love never held such meaning until the right person, the destined person, is able to show you every facet of that love, whether dark or fiery.

Numbness. Blockage. Distance. Nothing compared to what truly surrounded her when he stood before her. She cherished every gaze, every breath, every scent and as she looked into his eyes, she silently repeated, "Go away." Nothing justified her behavior. Fear is for fools, as is hope. The words etched deep into her subconscious now meant nothing, and she became a fool, devoured by fear.

Looking happiness straight in the eyes with a heart of stone, she said no. No to the happiness she had been waiting for these past few years in the darkness.

This weekend was supposed to change everything, it was supposed to be the turning point of their relationship, the moment of eternal union. Her home was meant to become his, his oasis to which he'd return—a place of desire, happiness, and love. A family.

She pictured every smallest detail in her mind, the gift she wanted to present to him was meant to be a testament of boundless love and devotion. A readiness to silently pledge the 'sacramental' promise, yes.

Giving him the keys to a place she held most dear in the world was, in her eyes, a complete willingness to give herself to him.

Fear prevailed and the home became a place he wanted to escape from as quickly as possible. What she saw in his eyes hurt more than banging her head against a wall. His sense of rejection, step by step, irrevocably sealed what they both had dreamed of.

He left.

The relationship still continued, but nothing was the same as before. That meeting had started to change everything. Do you remember? She asked herself. She didn't remember anything.

His kindness and love kept reminding her that he had to forgive her, that he understood why their last encounter went that way, he knew, he understood; yet, it hurt so much. Unconsciously, he was giving up, telling himself that it was too much, that he couldn't help her. Not when she herself kept saying she needed space, needed solitude. Leave.

Days passed, and the situation remained in limbo until the planned vacation didn't come to fruition. Once again, she had a chance to fix everything, but her selfish behavior and fears of the world closed off the last opportunity fate gave her.

She lay alone at home, slightly bruised from a car accident, nursing resentment toward the world and him for not being there with her. Why, knowing that he was suffering, did he choose a different trip? Why didn't he choose her?

She called, screamed, and insulted; hearing the same loving voice as always, repeating, soothing, that everything was fine, and it was her choice to go through it alone. She had said thousands of times not to come, that he couldn't, that it was better this way.

He complied with her order. He did what she wanted. He loved so deeply that he could deprive himself of happiness for her sake, just so she could be okay. But it wasn't enough for her. She left him.

That's the end.

Their separation was a matter of time. She did it under the influence of emotions, not realizing how much she had been mistaken that day.

He didn't have the strength to argue anymore, didn't have the strength for anything. She had drained everything out of him. He gave up.

Fine, I understand.

Through His Eyes

It was already too late for her to see everything through his eyes. Always thinking about herself, she never put herself in his shoes, for a moment not considering how much it cost him.

He crossed so many of his own barriers for her out of love. She didn't have a chance to reward him, to show him how much he meant to her and how much she owed him. She didn't have a chance to give him the true love he deserved.

From the perspective of passing time, she knew he had had enough. Love had crossed all permissible boundaries, broken him, and surprised him in matters where his certainty was stronger than thunder.

Acceptance is a wrong word, because you can accept a situation; he surrendered to it. Now, the small spark of her presence had become an essential element of his thoughts and words.

Learning more about her every day, consciously or not, they became a part of each other's lives. He loved her, and his entire love encompassed not only her but also her small existence.

Despite hiding it from him for so long, despite so much time having to pass before he got to know her, they were a trio, even though tangibly just a pair. They both knew about each other, expressing their interest in different ways.

His thoughts and questions about her were sincere and brimming with emotion. She, once again, the little being, expressed herself as best she could, drawing and translating dreams with colorful crayons, asking every time for him to receive it.

Childlike thoughts and actions, most sincere in their devotion. Genuine smiles and laughter with every phone call. Boundaries not worth dwelling on. He loved her with all the baggage she carried, with boundless love, supportive and pure like the whiteness of snow.

The girl with a baggage of experiences, not liberated from her past in the literal sense. The demons surrounding her and unresolved matters that stood in the way of their happiness. It weighed on him more than he could express.

Her feelings and well-being were paramount to him, and nothing that could hurt her or drive her into even greater guilt ever escaped his lips, even though it should have so many times.

What was his dream? Perhaps that's a question best asked in person, but everything that reached her later was so clear and vivid. He wanted her with all his might, he wanted to be with her for as much time as he could imagine.

The anticipation of their next meeting consumed him from the inside. Even though he loved her with an epic love, she rationed it out to him. Daily phone calls and messages were never able to completely fill the void within him.

The lack of touch, kisses, and a gaze filled with love and devotion, even though it was present, pushed him further away.

Every anticipated meeting, the moment he could see her, his heart pounding out of his chest. Brief moments with her, joy, laughter, magic. The gaze he bestowed upon her penetrated every part of her, and then he knew that she loved him like no one else ever had in his life.

His spoken words, those words, lifted her up. She was the only one in the world who gave him a love he had never felt before, she filled him. She took him with her despite the distance that separated them.

The possibility of feeling each other's warmth, the steady beating of hearts that had surrendered to each other for eternity. Pledged promises, spoken words, and gestures. That may only happen once in a lifetime.

The incomplete happiness that resided within him often tore him away from the embrace of love. The awareness that spoke to him, wanting something more, wanting more of her, started to make itself known.

Despite her repeated promises that everything would change, that things would work out, that they would be together more, she allowed him to come back and believe. She disappointed him, and he was left.

Farewells that shouldn't have been so many, that made tears flow down their cheeks, too often were tears of unhappiness, tears of longing, tears of emptiness that were approaching rapidly.

He had no control over her complete happiness, despite how much he wanted to make her happy, how much he wanted to give her a different life, she effectively blocked him, burning him out in the process. And when it might seem like both had accepted the situation as it was, he said it's over.

He lacked the strength so much, he was so defeated. With his head bowed, he walked away, leaving behind the person he loved with a kind of love the world had never seen.

I once heard that by truly loving someone, we must allow them to leave. But who in this story should leave? Her, allowing him to start living a full life, without drama, without expectations, without longing?

Or him, putting down his sword, should he give up in this unequal battle with her darkness?

The truth is that love works miracles. It lifts us when one falls, that love is elusive, that it propels us into actions that were never within our reach. Love is what makes us understand. Love pulls us out of the rubble of failure. Only when we lose it—

Return to the Abyss

For some, seven days make a week. For her, this week was meant to signify a new beginning. It was supposed to go smoothly and pleasantly. Just forget and move on. On the seventh day, there was no turning back anymore; everything became clear.

It's him, only he matters, she loves only him, and she will only love him. Nothing has ever become as certain as this one feeling.

Maybe just one phone call, one message, and everything will fall into place again. Maybe he'll understand and forgive again. After all, he loved her so much.

"Please come back, I'm sorry."

"No, don't you understand what happened? It's over, I can't go on like this."

That echoing in her head and the words repeating endlessly were like a dark mystical thread pulling her toward a place from which she knew very well there was no escape.

She screamed with a voiceless cry, tears flowing, falling deeper and deeper.

Days passed, each shaded in the same hues of gray and brown, she lived even though life had escaped her. A lifeless breath, an instinct forcing her to endure. Imaginations ending that piercing pain provided solace. Selfishness prevailed.

Have you ever heard the tale of a fallen princess who, like no one else, destroyed everything and everyone she loved the most? How the wicked queen filled her veins with poison, making her believe that the only thing she could do was inflict pain, reaping the same harvest for herself? Spiraling in a cycle of her own misery, much like a hamster in a wheel, she couldn't find a way out of it.

"Can you hear me? Please come back."

Did she say that? Multiple times but it was too late.

Time to start!

Loneliness, tears, longing.

"I have a girlfriend, I'm happy, she's similar to you."

"You forgot about me so quickly. What does she have that I don't?"

"Do you hear what you're saying?"

"How could you forget about me so quickly? You used to say I was the love of your life."

"I don't have to wait to see someone."

"I will wait, forever."

"I love you the most in the world, always only you."

That conversation kept playing in her mind, filling her from the inside. Every attempt to reach out ended the same way, the same words, the same rejection. He had forgotten about her already, stopped loving her.

"I don't love you anymore."

It hurt her so much, but her love never allowed her to stop loving. She loved now even more than ever, loved in solitude and suffering. She poured everything onto paper, feelings spilled out of her like from a bowl filled with tar, the same substance that held her captive for so many years. Once again, she felt like the cocoon from which she emerged was suffocating her even more than before.

It had become too much for her. Her continuous suffering for a love that was irretrievably gone felt like gray images flickering in the distance, unnoticed by anyone.

August 26th
My beloved,

I am so deeply sorry! With all my heart, I want to call you and tell you how much I regret and how much I apologize. I don't know why I keep putting off the phone call.

I'm so scared that if I love you even more than I do now, this love will eventually kill me. It's just so unreal that I can love someone so much, and that someone can love me just as strongly. Is it a miracle?

All my life, I believed that true love would never find me. But you, damn it, you changed everything! I still remember when we were sitting in the restaurant in our city, a city that will always be ours because it's where we met for the first time alone.

We talked about love, how it's always difficult, and there's never a happy ending. I told you that despite that, I'm still waiting for a prince from a fairy tale who will come on a white horse. Back then, I didn't know that this prince was sitting across from me!

You changed me. I really didn't want that, but you did it, only you succeeded! That's why I love you so much!

I know that another difficult time will come between us, but that's just how it is with us, right? 😊

I promise you that when this awful period in my life ends, you will feel my deep love for you again, and I will see all those feelings in your eyes that give us the strength to endure it.

Yours always.

I hope that despite my anger toward you right now, for going to your friend's thinking I don't want to see you and that I need space for myself, you know that you're my entire world!

I need you to know that, to know that it's true! EVERYTHING I need is you! Your gaze when things are bad kills me inside, because your eyes must be filled with happiness then, that's the real you! I love you with all my might and forever.

X

September 7th

My beloved!

Today is a terrible day but my heart doesn't want to stop loving you. All this time I need you so much, I miss you so much, no one can even imagine.

Today, you told me that you no longer love me. Damn it. Anything but that. I don't want to believe that it's true. You are everything I have, everything I love, everything I need.

Your smile, your eyes, your face when you're asleep. How you hug me, how you laugh even when I'm angry, how you start laughing at me when you don't have the strength for me anymore.

I love all of it more than anything in the world! I wake up every morning just to feel it again. Every day when I start with your message and a kiss, oh, the best feeling in the world that you can give me!

You are the perfect reason for all of this, and it's all so funny because I remember promising myself that no one would ever be as close to me as you are. I closed my heart to all the love and beautiful feelings, but you? I don't know how it happened that you got inside? I really don't know.

My best friend, when he was still alive, told me as we were heading home, "You can't live without love, you'll see, you'll fall in love and won't be able to live without that person anymore."

I laughed so much back then, but he said, "Someday, when you least expect it, someone will show up, and that true love will explain to you what I'm saying now."

Now, after years, I believe he already felt it then, that he was leaving and knew what was coming for me. Because he never spoke to me in that way. It was the only time I saw him like that and it was strange. Shortly after, he was gone.

I don't want to talk about it again because it's a nightmare that comes back to me every night. It's strange that now, when I need you the most in the world, I hear his voice every night, saying, "My little star, it's not a farewell, because love is like the wind, you can't see it, but you can feel it. Love will return when you open up. Fight against it." Damn bullshit, but there might be some truth in it when I hear that.

It doesn't matter! I really want to forget and remember only the good, beautiful moments and start everything anew with you, a new life only with you. Please come back to me! Come back to us.

I no longer know what a happy world looks like without you, I've never seen it. I was in darkness for so long, and you allowed me to come out of it. You showed me the beauty of love, happiness, and the world and I was so blind. Please come back.

I love you so deeply.
X

September 15th

So many empty weeks without you. How did all of this happen? I'm trying so hard to get back to you. Damn it. It's all so crazy. I'm so lost without you. I know I'm complicated, and I know it wasn't easy to be with me but you were. You endured.

You told me so many times that you love me so deeply and forever. I believed you in that.

You fully accepted my daughter, and you spoke of us as a family. We had dreams of growing old together in our garden, needing so many blue pills. Even now, thinking about it, I want to laugh so much, and I have a smile on my face.

Where did all of that go? Darling, you said you hadn't told anyone for so many years that you love them, what you feel. I want to remind you of those feelings, please!

You're the better part of me. My found piece of heart, the better half. I love you so incredibly deeply.

X

September 24th

Today. Your words. That you don't want me to come. Damn it, what pain, the same pain that tore my heart apart when you said you don't love me.

You know perfectly well it can kill me.

I deserve it after everything that happened in my life and what happened between us.

I want to see you so badly, feel your closeness. I want to breathe together with you again. I should stop.

Who in their right mind, after all of this, after such words, such important words, and especially after they were spoken by someone so important, still fights?

My beloved, my most wonderful man on earth, I still love you with all my might, and I can't imagine ever being able to stop. no part of my body wants to forget and stop.

I love you so incredibly deeply.
X

October 15th
Your name.

I don't know why I still write to you, it's so messed up, but I feel better when I do. I can't tell you all of this anymore, but I can pour it out of myself. Even if I were to tell you everything, I know it doesn't matter to you anymore. I tell myself that quietly, sobbing.

You've probably forgotten everything by now, us, me. You're probably in a happy relationship with someone else now. That thought kills me. But I want you to be happy. I dreamed that you would be happy with me, but I ruined everything. I was so selfish.

I love you with all my might, every day, I love you more and more. It's so terrifying for me. I close my eyes and I see you. I talk to you in my head every day. That photo of us, the one I have at home, the same photo I hid in the closet before you came. I don't know why?

I don't understand how I could. You and me. You and the little one. The two most important people in my life. My miracles in the world. I want to tell you a few things. That day when you were here.

When I waited for you so much, for so long. And when I became someone else. Not the person I should have been. I had a gift for you, so important to me, to us. I wanted to give myself to you completely, to give myself to you completely.

But.

I don't know exactly what the hell was wrong with me. I was so mean to you and you kept telling me how much you loved me. Even when you left.

I knew so many times, when you repeated that this distance is killing you, the waiting to see me. I wanted to change it so badly.

To wake up every day with you, to kiss you and make the day better, to wait for you to come home. I dreamed about it from the day we first saw each other in our city.

I promised you that I would cook a delicious meal when you visited, and when we sat in the kitchen, I was so eager to give you what I had prepared for you. Those were the keys to my oasis.

My home was supposed to become your home that day, you were supposed to know that I was ready and that I really only want you; our home.

This was supposed to be the last part of me, getting rid of the part where I ran away from feelings, where I hid when things were bad, where no one judged me. Because it was you, and only you, who accepted me completely, with all my flaws, with my daughter, and with all the crap that always surrounded me.

I made such a big mistake in my life. I should have given this to you, even if you were going to say something bad. Because you were, you are, and you always will be worth it.

I wish I could tell you that I'm ready now to do everything for us, to be together every day. I'm not weak anymore, I'm not afraid anymore but now it's all too late.

I really wish I could see that you're different, that everything changes. That you'll come back. I'll always have hope.

You don't know how much I could do to give you one last chance, to give us that last chance. I'll wait for you for the rest of my life! No one else, just you, the love of my life!

Every day, I'll do everything to make you see that! It won't be words that matter, but actions! I'll regain your great love and I'll never expose it to all of this again. You'll feel it again, what you said. That you never felt that someone loved you so deeply.

Please, if you can hear me now, I'll fix this. I promise! Let me give you everything you need, because you deserve it more than anyone else in the world. See that it's only you, you've always been the only one!

You will know the real me. Full of happiness and love. only love. Never tears.

I would really love for us to find the light together. Our shared path of life. No matter where you want to go, I'll always follow you.

Let me be with you again, let us be with you. I love you with all my strength. Every day stronger and stronger.

If you only let me come back, I promise on my life that you will be the happiest in the world. I've waited for you my whole life, and I've never been so sure of it as I am now. Everything is so clear and bright.

YOU ARE THE LOVE OF MY LIFE FOREVER! EVEN WHEN I TAKE MY LAST BREATH, THAT FINAL BREATH WILL BE JUST FOR YOU.

It doesn't matter if we spend half a day together, one night, what matters is that we'll be close together again, that we'll breathe together again and our hearts will beat as one.

I love you with all my strength forever.
X

A small moment, just a small moment was enough. After writing the last letter, which happened to fall on her birthday, she took the phone in her hand and without much thought, dialed his number.

She didn't even expect that after everything, he would send her birthday wishes. Just the usual, cold 'happy birthday'. For her, they were like the trigger of memories. Memories, pain.

At that moment, she wanted to hear his voice the most. This day was supposed to be one of the happiest days, she dreamed that for the first time, she would spend her birthday with the person who meant the most to her in the world. Nothing could be further from the truth.

Loneliness. Pain. Sadness. Memories. Suffering. Words that etch their own decalogue, which every day was engraved deeper into her soul.

The words she used in the conversation with the most wonderful man in the world didn't reflect at all what she truly felt from the beginning. With her behavior, was she hoping for sympathy? A bit of breaking through the stony heart he had become toward her?

He, strong and heartless, devoid of any feelings for her, calmly listened to every mumbling word she said. Not giving her even a shred of hope in a single second that something remained in him. That somewhere far away, a small piece of her love still lingered within him.

"You know, in order to fix someone, you really have to fix yourself first. But how do you fix something that has already ceased to exist?"

"You are the love of my life. I've been waiting for you my whole life. Through good and bad."

Did it cease to exist because it never truly existed? Because we hear what we want to hear? And we say what others want to hear from us?

She thought that nothing worse could happen, that the only thing she had to deal with was the struggle to survive without him. To learn how to live without him. Fate mocked her once again.

The message that fell on her completely shattered her sense of any justice. Dad. Another hospital stay, another fight for life. She had to call him. she had to hear his voice again, she had to tell him how hard it was for her, how much she needed him now, when her beloved dad's life was hanging in the balance.

Crying and lamentation echoed through the phone, and she stutteringly tried to get him to help her. Despite everything that had happened between them, she could still count on him.

Even after their confessions, their pleas for a return, he was no longer hers, but he was there, supporting her, listening, giving her words of comfort. What mattered was that he answered. She heard his voice, and for a moment, he had the strength to fight.

"Everything will be okay, you're strong. You have to believe that it will be okay."

"He can't leave me either."

"Everything has accumulated at once. Damn it, but it will be okay."

"Please, you've been and still are more than just a partner to me. I could tell you everything. Don't leave me now."

"I won't leave, I'm—you're strong, I believe in you."

He knew what was tangled up in her life, and even though he would rather forget, he didn't turn away from her. She loved him even more for that, and it became even harder for her to cope with everything.

The day the doctor said during the hospital visit that there was nothing more to be done, and all that remained was waiting, she broke down. She knew that another man in her life would soon have to leave.

She already knew then that her end was also approaching. She felt like a dark, viscous tar that pulled her into an abyss, overwhelming her every day, surrounding her and taking away every breath.

She returned home with only one thought. Only he could calm her down, only his voice for a moment would give her solace.

"What happened? Why are you crying again?"

"Dad."

"What happened?"

"They said there's nothing more they can do."

"Damn it. Calm down. Tell me what's happening."

"He doesn't even hear me, he doesn't even know I was there, he doesn't even feel how I held his hand."

"He knows you're there, you'll manage."

"He can't leave me either. You, him. My friend. I won't be able to handle it."

"Calm down, let's talk about something—"

"I want you to come back. I need you so much right now. I'm sorry I called you, but only with you can I talk about this. I need you."

"Damn it."

"I'm sorry, I want to fix everything so badly. Please don't leave me now."

"I'm here, you can always call."

"Will you let me fix everything if you're alone again? I promise I'll do everything."

"I don't know what the future holds."

These conversations had no end, continuous pleading intertwined with tears. The last conversation they had was the least pleasant, when he said he didn't want to see her anymore, didn't want anything to do with her anymore. She should forget.

Hearing his voice now feels like driving her to madness, he has a girlfriend and he's happy, comparing her to someone else in his eyes. The overwhelming feeling that there's someone who can replace her burned her from within.

The screams and shouts she heard from him, she knew they signaled the end of everything. That she wouldn't be able to call, talk, that there's no rescue left. She only managed to tell him that one day, coming back home, her little daughter asked her why she was so sad.

She couldn't tell such a young child that her beloved grandfather might soon pass away, she only said that there were things mommy couldn't handle and couldn't fix.

Looking at her, the child said, "Mommy, who always tells me that we're strong and can handle everything, that when we really want something, we can always find a way to get it?"

She could suspect everything but not this; that her own child's words, aimed at her, would ricochet and leave such a mark on her, and that this moment would be pivotal for her and for everyone involved.

On the same day, she hit rock bottom, drowning like a wretched soul. She did what she did best—killed the emotions and feelings within her. She fell, reaching out for help.

Her friend, who valiantly stood by her side, now replacing the absent father, saw her state and how they were regressing back to the past, and said enough.

She called the only person who could offer her support at that moment, the person who could make such an impact on her in her eyes. It was her last attempt at salvation. Like an emergency response team, her late friend's mother appeared at her door.

No one else patted her head, no one else gave their approval and permission for her to end this way. It had to end now, right there in that moment, when both of them stood before her and she gave in.

The mother of her late friend dealt her the most powerful blow, slapping her cheek and shouting that enough is enough, that her son didn't leave for her to follow suit, that this all needs to stop, that she's had enough of watching both of them go away. As she left, slamming the door, she took her friend with her, leaving her alone.

She needed this moment more than air at that time. She felt like she was hit by a snowball, like she was literally left alone. Trying to shake off what had just happened, the words of her little daughter suddenly returned to her mind.

The fight had just begun.

Whenever you close your eyes, your mind knots, and you imagine what could happen. You create various scenarios in your head, envisioning your own story, but do you truly bring them to life? No, why? Because you don't know how.

The answer is often simple, yet you can't see it written down in the diagnosis on the pages of your own mind. It's all fear. We prefer someone else to make decisions for us, so we can later use them as a scapegoat for all the mess; she wasn't any different.

She blamed everyone, forgetting about herself, lost in her selfish pain, blind to the pain of others, to their experiences, their losses, and struggles.

Do you think he didn't fight? He did; without saying a word to her, he fought every day for himself. His own demons consumed him more than he could admit; why? Because of her blindness.

She never allowed herself to truly see that he had lost more in life than she did. Not a great move. You recall the first words about selfish women unable to admit their own failures, constantly hiding behind his dark shadow.

A textbook example. Even the heart attack of the most fragile being on earth won't change the fact of how destructive we are as a species, to ourselves and the environment around us.

Because where should her attention be focused? How much on her experiences, and how much on his. Because this damn thing called love is such, it doesn't reveal its true face from the beginning, only after a loss does it inform us of its real nature.

She

Who was she, really? It's hard to say. She herself didn't truly know for a long time, didn't know her purpose, her direction. She was searching for her own path. Searching.

It might sound prosaic to say that she was born for a certain purpose, and maybe that was the case, but she struggled for a long time to uncover it.

Do you sometimes see how the world around you lives its life, yet you don't fit into it in any way, not because you don't belong, but because you can't fully immerse yourself in it?

You do everything that the society and the reality of that time dictate, but you realize that you're just a puppet in this grand void? And every person you meet on your path teaches you a lesson that offers a chance for change, yet you can't seem to make use of it in any way? Sound familiar? Probably.

It's nonsense to listen to people who have always known who they want to be and what they need to achieve. They've worked it out for themselves to satisfy others, but in reality, all of us need to work for it.

Fall a million times to get up a million times and search again but we'll find it because nature loves equilibrium. She learned this the hard way. and even though she knew her life wasn't a fairytale from a hundred-acre wood, she always, despite failures, tears, and sorrow, managed to find one small valuable thing for which she could be grateful.

And like a drowning person clinging to a life preserver, she held onto that small find to make it through another day.

Sometimes, they were minimalisms in their smallest form, and sometimes, they were just words taken out of context. but how did she learn to live? That the power of thought can turn into what we want because we are born like a clean white sheet of paper, untouched by ink.

At first glance, with bigger or smaller possibilities of the surrounding reality. But how many times has history shown that to become a valuable, fulfilled person, you don't need millions, just perseverance, which we all lack?

If I told you that on her journey, in moments of greatest fear, people started appearing, acting like rescue services, providing her with oxygen when she was breathless, would you believe me? No and do you know why? Because you wouldn't be looking in that direction.

Dare to look, and perhaps everything will start to resemble a well-crafted pattern worthy of your attention, which will eventually transform into the field of your battle. And remember, when you take up the fight, there's no turning back. You fight until you win.

One phone call, one sometimes poorly thought-out moment, might allow you to find something you didn't even know you needed so much. An open mind and belief in another person will enable all of that, you just need not belief. Not hope.

You need an impulse and the last thing you'd have thought you needed. Crazy, isn't it? I know.

There are so many matters, so many things of which we have no idea, and once upon a time, we didn't believe in them either. She was among those skeptics but she stopped being one.

Because the woman who didn't allow her to doubt for a moment, who extracted from her everything that could help her let him go, try to forget. All of that was built as her internal survival strength.

Listen. When you talk to someone you don't know, someone who knows you; strange, knows everything about you, knows more about your life than she knew about herself. She gave her hope, often not holding back her words. She taught her but also detached her. Why?

Yes. If at any point reading her story, you sympathized with her, was it wrong? There's no place for sympathy for her. It's a place for acknowledgment for him. Sympathy for him, that despite everything, he loved her. Selfish and so very weak.

He loved her despite her hurting him every day. Her behavior only built her own ego. She elevated her pedestal to an unimaginable scale of self-admiration and self-punishment. Why? So many questions.

Because she didn't know any other way, and only he pointed out her path. For a happy path, every battle must start within oneself. She had to stop acting subconsciously for the sake of others. To consciously provide happiness, she had to finally think about herself, not in a selfish way, but in a healing way.

It's the worst to love and not know whether you're truly loved in return. People grab onto anything when they're sinking. Damn paradox. She denied herself and her child everything just to pay a little to the person who could have kept her alive.

With that fucking hope that maybe everything would really work out, that it was just a whirlwind. She didn't know what she should have known by then, she didn't realize how deeply she had ensnared herself in a cycle of self-destruction.

Alcohol again became an essential companion in her everyday life. What was she thinking back then? What was she feeling? Damn emptiness, sadness, regrets, longing, moments when she desperately tried to remind herself how much she loved him.

She knew that no matter what anyone did or thought, everything was still in his hands. She was like a damn puppet manipulated by strings in his sense of nothingness. As if there was some sort of magical button for quickly turning off emotions, it's amazing how much she could have accomplished back then.

One small fragment from a day of nothingness. Not his day, but hers. You wait for something that you never really know will happen, you believe in it with all your might, you take blows, yet you remain so blind to the reality that surrounds you.

You have to remain blind to survive. You don't know what's truly true, what you should really do. She didn't know either. She only knew that the love she had was slowly killing her. It hurt, not just emotionally; that love began to hurt her physically as well.

Medical bullshit about nerve pain. No, that's not it. It's not about nerve pain, it's about the love that remained trapped in some way. Why? However it can be explained, she only explained it in one way.

Maybe there's truly some mystical energetic connection that allows her to feel what he's truly feeling. Or maybe it's just her own fears, her darkest scenarios that were crying out for justice. I don't know.

Imagine what she felt every day. She closed her eyes, lit candles in some inexplicable way to connect with him, to feel what he felt, to read all those unspoken words, those thoughts smoldering inside him and what did she get after every conversation with him? The thing she feared the most.

That there would be someone who not only questioned her feelings for him, but also his feelings for her little one. Oh, someone who's damn selfish and a symbol of their own unsuccessful life, showing a bloody sign of unfulfillment, who would say that it's wrong, that he loves a child who isn't his.

Disgusting? Indeed. How so many pretend care and friendship, often hurting that person with their selfish approach. Because it takes immense courage on his part to admit how much he loves her daughter.

How important she is to him. A true hero, a true person of value can do that, while all the others are often just pathetic, tender beings trapped in their feelings of worthlessness. He was different. Why? Because he was exceptional. He is.

That's why he's so worthy of love, so worthy of everything. One thing I can say about him, about her, is that in all that suffering, in all that longing, in all that chaos, they experienced the greatest happiness by finding each other even though they often thought differently.

Even though many times, both of them tried to let go. True love is truly put to the test. To fight, to shed tears, to endure suffering.

What did she think every day? Thoughts crowded her mind. She fought and stumbled. She didn't know how to live. She tried, she loved, and it was killing her but she'll always be with him. Hope isn't the last thing to die. Love doesn't die last, but not when the body leaves.

She was exactly that. Enigmatic, internally self-conscious girl with big dreams, with fulfilled love in her heart, waiting for her time. A girl who, more than once, hid her true feelings behind her behavior, fearing and fighting.

Tough? No. Internally fragile. Shouting. She simply didn't understand. Unhappy without him. Nothing more, or perhaps everything. And how did others see her? The truth isn't always colorful. And now, hear about her in the voice of the crowd.

"Complex personality, yet incredibly noble. I don't know why, but she usually got what she set her mind to, making every one of us envious. Yet, with her, it was a paradox in her behavior.

"All of us were striving for recognition, career, and all those material things, and she had them, of course she worked hard for them, but it all came to her with such ease that it was almost incomprehensible.

"She valued it greatly, but even knowing her, she wouldn't have made a pros and cons list just to give it all up to be happy. I remember one thing she said at a party when some guys were bragging about their earnings and status.

"She stood up and loudly said, 'Bullshit, happiness can't be bought.' That's her in her entirety, ostentatious in her statements and behavior, unable to tolerate shallow talk."

"In my whole life, I probably only know her, who with full responsibility, would live under a bridge with her love just to come back after a day of collecting scrap and feel loved and important to that person. That's exactly how extreme she is." K.

"Ha-ha. Her (laughter) I'd most like to say that she's someone you either love or hate (laughter) even though she has a golden heart, just try entering her space or doing something that might hurt someone close to her, and she won't bat an eye before destroying you. That's why I adore her." M.M.

"I remember an incident from our youth (laughter); we were sitting in one of the pubs and a few guys joined us (laughter), everyone except her was thrilled, that's how it looked when you went out with her, either you knew something would happen or you went out without her, doomed to boredom."

"Because when she used to go out with us before all this. (Thoughtful pause.) What happened to her, it was always like a magnet, everyone approached. With a flicker of her innate sarcasm, she chased them away so quickly that the guys' didn't even understand what she meant, leaving politely and smiling."

"I still envy her for that and try to learn it myself, to say something like that with such grace, with that twinkle in her eye, that the opponent falls in love immediately while also feeling the excitement of being outsmarted. That's her all over." E.

"I don't know what's going on with her now. I tried writing, but I know her, she'll want to call. Earlier? (Thoughtful pause.) Crazy but you know, in a positive way, although not always."

"You see, it was like that, but it's either black or it's white, and there was nothing in-between with her. So, when I messed up once, you think there was any talk? She chewed me out like a dog, but I didn't owe her anything (laughter)."

"Although I remember her telling me once, maybe because she either ran out of arguments or just didn't feel like talking to me anymore, to read a dictionary and start using words when I understand their meaning (laughter)."

"She was nuts, but now when you ask me and how I think of her, I hope, and damn it, I know that in many matters, I can still count on her." G.

"Her name. Interesting and not very common. I remember when I asked her not to be called Beatka, I guess I felt that she wouldn't be an ordinary person. Even though I was young, my intuition didn't fail me."

"From a very young age, she stood out among other children. She never had to try too hard to achieve something. I was impressed by that. In fact, it's still the same today. The goals she sets for herself, she always achieves. It's not always without losses though."

"Losses in this case are the personality traits she acquired. The sense of infallibility, the 'I know better' attitude, is an indispensable companion for her. I did it, I achieved it, I want. I know better. Because it's all me."

"It certainly reinforces her chosen direction. Unfortunately, she often overlooks the people who were with her as she achieved it all. Those people are just 'bodies', stepping stones to the goal. Almost reaching the goals, but where are the people?"

"It's like a proverbial scale. The scale has its pans. It's hard to balance them evenly on your own. That's probably why she swings to extremes. Sometimes she's loving and sweet, and other times she's arrogant and unpleasant."

"One thing is for sure, you can always count on her. She won't refuse help, even in the middle of the night. She needs balance, someone who will keep the scales evenly weighted on the scale." Sis.

"She is an incredibly intelligent, resourceful, and independent person. She doesn't like having superiors or dictators over her. She's goal-oriented and strives for a high standard. She doesn't always take the advice of others, although she always listens, but in the end, she'll do things her way."

"Many times, she's as relentless as hell, sensitive, which adds to her charm and radiance. She's like fire and water. Seeking a love that would accept all of that. If someone crosses her path and tries to harm her, speak ill of her or her loved ones, she can bring that person down to the depths. It's better not to start anything (laughs)." Mom.

"Please. She can't be described in a few words. I know her briefly but at first glance; a corporate bitch, around whom you have to watch every word. Second glance; a person who can sort everything out for everyone, even if she can't, she'll find out, won't give up, and will sort it out."

"Third glance; a rock that can straighten out your life in five minutes and one conversation, give it meaning, and support you at every stage of change. Looking at her, you get the impression that all of this comes to her with such ease, it's obvious and simple."

"Walking self-assuredness, calmness, and sophistication. You break through the first layer, and there are millions of thoughts, tangles of emotions, and an unwanted sea of empathy." P.

The way others perceive her as nonsense, when she herself doesn't see anything extraordinary in herself. Sense of self-worth. Without the bullshit, omitted in every human existence.

Perhaps only those so tiny and deeply insecure are capable of admitting how much they value themselves. But the truth looks different. That great one who doesn't see greatness within himself. He didn't see it either. And he was great. Is. Will be. Until the end.

About him?

He

So many words have been said. So many descriptions, so many confessions. So.

It won't happen. Why?

Because he gave her love. He gave her himself and all that he experienced. All that he felt. All that he lost. All that he fought for. He entrusted it to her until the secret grave.

Maybe someday.

Certainly not now.

Because the word promise, vow, is more precious than gold. He trusted her.

And she won't lose that trust.

Not when it comes to what the past etched in him, like a tattoo etched into bone.

My love, you're safe. I'll die before I let you perish.

Feelings?

Feelings? There are two ways to write about it now. Why? Feelings are something she renounced, something she learns every day with varying degrees of success. Her silver lining in misfortune is that she found people who always provide her with advice.

They help, they prophesize. Every evening, she tries to find an inner voice that could guide her even in the smallest way, telling her what she should really do. On the edge, falling and yet rising.

It's impossible to write about her feelings, it's impossible to explain even in some metaphorical way what's really happening inside her. She herself probably doesn't understand it the best.

She loves and at the same time, she's haunted. Not by him. More by herself. More by the fact that she can't find her place in the situation she's in. Her entire awareness now gains the title of the deepest darkness, the farthest beginnings of a messed-up mess. But she knows one thing.

No matter what, she will still love. She will punish herself and endure his punishment. All the bitter words, all the seeds of indifference, in a second, she'll be able to let them fade into oblivion just to gain a single moment of happiness she's been waiting for.

She has strength, even though she shouldn't have any left, even though so many voices of her own consciousness suggest that this isn't the right way. That every woman, blah blah. Should be pursued, fought for but is that really the case?

Now, the voices of feminists fighting for their freedom and independence come to the forefront. (Laughter.) They're the ones who all say the same thing, not this way.

Fuck the straight path. The more twisted it is, the funnier it gets, right? Well, that's exactly what the strength of her messed-up personality suggests every day. On one hand, she's not a proper romantic, on the other, a split-second realist.

Why split-second? Because the longer she hesitates about whether she's acting right, the quicker she'll fall into another self-destruction, as if what she's been through so far wasn't enough.

Going back.

She loves him, period. She gave him her heart. She gave him her soul. That's how she decided, and that's how she'll live. Maybe it won't be an ideal life written in romantic prose or fiction, but it will be some kind of life.

She'll definitely be able to say one thing. I lived and experienced passionate love in my life. Was she just an option for him? Damn right, more than once. Did she know? Of course.

Does that mean she didn't respect herself? Well, it depends on how the fuck you look at it. Getting to know this hysteria, trying to understand what's going on. I see one thing. It wasn't a lack of self-respect that drove her, it wasn't the years of learning to carry a thorny crown that were so deeply etched into her.

She wanted more and more not because she didn't know how to live without pain, but something deeper was at play. Only a truly empathetic person with a profound understanding won't judge. In my opinion, something led her that not many people in the world possess.

That something is the deeply human instinct to see in others what even that person can't see in themselves. What is it? Goodness. Nobility. Pain. Wounding. Internal struggle.

Funny? Truly, very much so. Those who haven't experienced suffering and loss won't understand. She, probably seen by most now as a victim, an unconditional being, her feelings tossed in the trash like a piece of used paper, along with the twists of life.

That's a mistake because I admire her every day. The lessons from her story wash over me every time I think of it. And even though she's pushing her boulder uphill like Sisyphus, without a shred of imagination whether she'll succeed, she believes, loves, and waits and only death can be stronger.

Although having gone through her whole story, I believe that even death won't stop her. I wish that for myself.

And what do I wish for him? You could say that I wish he would see the light, but there's no point in wishing for him because, in my eyes, he has everything. He just needs the courage, not the courage to fight, but the courage to say out loud to himself that the thrown words have already gained meaning.

You can't influence someone else's will, but you can influence your own. That's what I wish for him. And although you could say, as long as there's time, before it's too late; in this matter, there's no reflection.

Because her love is eternal, and even though there's so much left to desire, so many words left unspoken, and so many words spoken too many times, I sincerely believe that such exceptional people are put through this trial not because they can, but because they are capable.

Only they can bear it, learn from it, and then teach others with their greatness, so that their voice resonates loudly in the afterlife, and the wave carries everyone. I'm not just talking about feelings, love, and overrated romance here. but about every sphere of life.

A dense wave of suffocating thoughts, seeking an outlet and perhaps some comfort. A person who could become responsible for the course of events, a companion of helplessness.

She could call it a friend of fear and downfall. A friend of failure and strength. She longed for happiness, happiness for herself, happiness and fulfillment. The whirlwind of her thoughts and vibrations of her own ignorance in finding meaning in the situation only delivered more blows, like a sword to her heart or the organ that should be in its place.

Waiting for a better tomorrow; sad but true. Each new day could be the better one, the more splendid one. Treat this day as if there won't be any more after it, as if there's only now and here.

Easy? No. Damn difficult. The hardest, but that's what fighting means. Fight.

Phoenix

Do you know that feeling when you open your eyes and the world suddenly seems different? Do you see something you've never noticed before? Do you smell scents that were never apparent to you before?

Have you ever felt the obligation to do something to prove not to the world, but to yourself, that you're not just a fragile little being, but a resilient example of survival?

She felt that.

Throughout the night, she searched the internet for help, for solutions. She reached out to every connection that came to mind, regardless of whether she was walking into the lion's den or not.

What she would have to give up to get closer to her goal didn't matter. She promised on her life that she would save him and steadfastly fulfilled her vow. The number of messages she sent to specialists, describing her father's struggles and attaching countless files, seemed endless.

The lack of response didn't frighten her; it motivated her even more. Even if she had to kiss the devil, she was ready to do it. After all, they already knew each other quite well.

There's an answer.

She called him with the news that she had found a specialist who was willing to undertake the treatment and rescue of her father. She fought persistently to make it happen.

That's very good news, I'm really happy, everything will be fine, you just have to believe in it.

Today is the day, the most important day for her father. Today will determine whether all the efforts were not in vain. It's the day that will show how much strength she had within her, how much she wanted it to succeed.

The day she shouted to herself that no one would leave her again in her life. She set out on a journey for them to meet at the destination, where new life would be breathed into him. Hours of waiting caused thoughts to swirl in her head.

Thoughts not only about her father, who was now the most important purpose of her existence. But thoughts revolving around him, to call him as soon as possible and tell him everything. She had so much to say to him, so many moments she wanted to share with him.

Every time his memory came to her thoughts, an irresistible and inexplicable pain tore through her chest from within. Every memory seemed so fresh, as if it happened just yesterday.

She loved him more than anything in the world and desired his happiness. She lied to herself. She lied to him in every conversation, saying that if he could be happy without her that would be enough for her.

Only he matters, and what he wants. A crappy rule she used to keep herself somewhat human and normal, thereby expressing her readiness for friendship.

It was all her gift. She learned to see what wasn't visible. Building the strength of her own character, the will of someone else's life. She wasn't a god, she couldn't make miracles tangible.

But she loved and the strength of her love showed what she was capable of, even though she remained so blind to it. She saved him. With each heartbeat, a new beginning was born.

He recovered, returned and she didn't break the promise she screamed silently to herself. She will never lose anyone again. Just believe that there's no one stronger.

Her amazement was even greater when the unexpected improvement in her relationship with her mother heralded a new true beginning. Those invisible signs. Words screamed in pain. Reverberated from the depths of her own subconscious.

All those years of living in darkness. Spitting out tar. Ignited with the spark of a certain kind of justice. We are what we allow ourselves to be and she would never allow herself to be weak again, not anymore.

November 7th

Another day of fighting for life, fighting to breathe, fighting to feel. Nothing heralded the impending end of the world, nothing gave such a strong indication that it could be so bad and yet.

"When I hear your voice, I'm on the brink of going crazy. You're important to me, but I have to move on. You'll manage."

The never-ending voices in her head during the conversation with him. That piercing sorrow, that sadness, and perhaps shed tears. The incomprehensibility of the spoken words not wanting to be so deeply embedded in her mind.

The impossibility of stopping loving from one day to the next. It all seemed like a damn reconstruction of some psychedelic movie. Why? Was this love so immense that it exceeded the other person?

In hindsight, it seems to me that it was, and every subsequent event increasingly confirmed it, even though the reader remained blind to the read lines for so long.

I won't give up, even though I should have so many times. She kept telling herself that every time, promising that she would never take a step toward him again. Luckily for her, she could keep her promises only for a moment.

Fate and inexplicable attraction didn't allow her to do otherwise. The beginning had no end, and the end was an undefined unknown, heading toward endless nothingness, waiting for the moment of awakening.

Breathe. This Is
Just the Beginning

She mentioned earlier about her readiness for friendship. What a crappy, senseless, and prosaic word; friendship. She, who knew unconditional friendship, had the courage to talk to the love of her life about a shared friendship.

No one could come up with a bigger load of crap, not even the most drugged person in the world. The truth is, we will never form a friendship with someone who is the love of our life.

We will never offer support unconditionally. Envy, all-encompassing, will always make itself known. Cynicism spread here in its truest form.

When you love with the greatest and sincerest love in the world, never turn away from what surrounds you. Observe, because around every corner something awaits to be sent by fate to fuel your belief in a better tomorrow. Don't give up, because the unexpected is on its way.

It arrived. The day that was meant to gradually transform her perspective on her longing, her sadness, her sorrow, her emptiness, was finally meant to turn into a fight. And she was/is the most valiant in the world.

She fought her whole life and she pursued her dreams her whole life. Life itself wanted to show her that there are no impossible things, all you need is to want. All you need is patience. All you need is one small gesture to know that it's worth it.

One message revealed her deeply hidden will to fight. The battle began that evening when someone completely unknown but not unknown to him found out how darkness took everything from her.

That one question, "Is it not worth waiting for a miracle?" It's worth it. The most in the world, it's worth it.

Metaphorical conversations about darkness, the emerging light. The depths that engulf a person and extract the smallest fragments of humanity from them, statements like 'hope is for fools' led to deeper and more meaningful conversations.

"You know, it's worth believing in miracles. Regardless of how impossible they may seem."

A miracle gives you something intangible, as if blessing your efforts. Hope, on the other hand, is just hope. You often do something in vain, because despite your efforts, it doesn't reward you with anything. That's what hope is like. it makes you do something without giving anything in return.

Remember, faith has no limit. it's easy to lose it, but harder to find it again.

There's no point. The drawers closed after years. There's no need to invite demons back. Do you know what it's like to be in a dream for years, from which you can't wake up? Until finally feeling that it's enough?

You wake up, you do it just like that, as if those years didn't exist. You lost so much time, but in the end, you forgive yourself. A strange feeling.

The ability to forgive oneself is a great thing. Not everyone is capable of it. Many don't even realize they're in the dark and that things can be different. Respect to her for managing to forgive herself. A noble trait that many lack.

Referring to that saying. It's not a skill, it's rather courage. Look; you're at the bottom, so deep that hurting yourself doesn't even pain you anymore, you've perfected self-punishment and the slow path of self-destruction, you lie at the bottom but see a different world through different eyes.

You're just scared to get up and walk toward that world, fearing that what put you at the bottom will be lost and forgotten. That memory will fade. But you stand up, courage pushes you toward what your eyes see, what you've been resisting.

And now you want it like never before. But you can only get it under one condition. Finding the courage within you to look yourself in the face and say. I FORGIVE MYSELF. I WANT TO LIVE. Would you get up?

I think it would take a while. I'd delay it. Why did this sudden decision to get up come about? To leave the darkness, cast off the chains? What happened?

Initially, it wasn't a conscious decision. Not one she made herself. A simple question and the answer seems trivial. You see, no one likes stepping out of their comfort zone, especially not this person.

Despite genuinely hating the place she was in, she felt strangely safe there because, after all, what could be worse? But you see. That was a mistake in her thinking. Sometimes, a little light appears in the dark, you extinguish it, and it keeps coming back, but if one day you extinguish it and it doesn't return, you go out to find it.

You selfishly extinguish it and now you're trying to relight it with the last match. You have only one chance in a million. Will you fight?

What is that little light?

Don't try to figure it out.

Did you take off your crown of thorns?

Finally, yes. Funny.

Barely a week separated her from his birthday, and she knew there was almost no chance they would spend it together, but she knew, she felt that she had to do something because she needed to see if the spark could blind her with its brightness and provide a tangible reason, a tangible reason to fight.

One chance. Only one to know. One carefully planned gift. She had to know. She had to feel that he would remember. She had to know that he still loved her. She had to know. If there was anything left in him, she had to see it.

A plan took shape in her mind, the most perfect plan she could imagine, the strength she had found within herself, fueled by the recent shades of faith, to do something that could, step by step, reverse everything that had been happening to her recently.

Her little being, who had loved him from the moment of their first meeting, who had created his presence in her life like a brave warrior, stood by her side, ready to fight. To fight for a better time. To fight for love. To fight for him. always and forever.

Just as you close your eyes and imagine how your life could look. As you recall all the happiest moments of your life, as you suddenly feel those kisses that touch; the most tender touch that only that one person can give, you lose yourself.

Her feelings were never as strong as they were on that day. That day changed everything for her. Did he already know that this day had changed him too?

November morning, nervously preparing to hear his velvety voice, full of swirling mysteries around him. So familiar to her, yet so enigmatic at the same time. Because if dreams come true, she knows what she should dream about because it's worth living for someone and not just for oneself.

She will never close her eyes when she looks into his face. Her silent hope that this morning will show her everything. Answer all her questions. Reveal the colors.

"Happy birthday, can we call you?" He couldn't have expected what she had prepared for him.

That short moment, waiting for the dull sounding signals to finally end and he appears on her screen, her heart stopped, her breath quickened, and her body became nervous.

Imagine being someone who was loved like no one else in the world on one hand, and on the other hand, a person who undertook a battle. A battle she intended to win at all costs.

Two beings who waited for him to reveal even a fragment of what he has within, so they would know that the fight makes sense.

"Happy birthday to you all," they shouted, holding a cupcake with a lit birthday candle, symbolizing a birthday cake. "Make a wish and blow it out."

The battle began right then and there. The moment when the face she knew so well, defending itself in every way, showed her what she had been waiting for, what she feared she wouldn't see again.

That glimmer, that look. Those eyes.

Words are like paper, they can take anything, and he could have said anything he wanted, he could have hurt her with words as much as he wanted. But the look in his eyes, his expression; no one could deceive her.

Colors like a rainbow wave surged in. An irresistible gust of returning warmth of hope filled every fiber of her being. Seeing him after such a long time. She knew he was still there. His love for her was still there, buried in the deepest layers of his heart but it was there.

The gaze that accompanied that conversation, the emotion, the struggle within himself, it was enough for her to know then that she had to do everything to regain what was hers.

You stand on the edge of a great abyss. The most beautiful place surrounds you on all sides. Colors of the sky intertwine. Shades of pink, orange. Saturated blue. You feel the scents that numb your body.

The taste of sweetness on your lips. The depth of light that eagerly calls you, inviting you in. You close your eyes and lose yourself. You already know you're where you should be. You've found your place on Earth.

He was hers, and she was his. That day changed everything. The story began anew. A battle, the toughest battle to fight.

"Don't wonder if she won this battle. She still fights. Only death can stop her. For a love that happens only once. About souls of karmic destiny. You can never stop fighting. It's a war being waged."

"And every battle brings her closer to her goal. Do you think she'll win this battle? Or has hope truly become the mother of fools? Are you wondering if this story could have really happened? Wait."

"Do you remember the darkness? Do you remember the pervasive darkness? Do you remember the safety? Do you remember the thorns she bore? The tarry abyss that consumed and called to her vanished like a sandcastle built on the shore."

"Now close your eyes. She doesn't remember it anymore. It doesn't carry her to sleep. One. Two. Three. She breathes. She's back. His invisible hand pulled her drowning body from the abyss. I am. I'm coming. Are you waiting?"

"SHE WAS SO WRONG. Is hope the realm of fools? She was a fool. Hope, it quenched her with a new light of life."

"Remember. Only it holds us in the greatest moments of doubt. You can doubt everything but never doubt hope. As long as you have it in your heart, there's nothing stopping you from pursuing your dreams."

"No gratitude was meant to be. I have to."

*MY LOVE, THANK YOU. I HAVE SUCH A LONG
FIGHT AHEAD. THANK YOU.*
I'M ALIVE.
FOR YOU
THANKS TO YOU
FOR YOU
FOR ALL OF YOU
ALWAYS AND FOREVER.

*It's thanks to the love for you, it's thanks to how you
showed me the world, the meaning of life. The colors of
love. I could close everything that remained open. Thanks
to you, there was a farewell.*

*Meet the new me. Yet so old. Know me as you never had
the chance to know me. You loved me in the dark. Love me
again in the light.*

Yours forever.
X.

The Game Has Just Begun

It was like a dream. Damn, what a dream. It was a coma, a bomb with delayed detonation. Did it explode? No. It's about to explode.

And then the darkness will be covered with fire, a small spark ignited by an invisible ray of a hidden gaze in one gesture will fall exactly where hot bubbling bubbles repeatedly breathed, pushed away by the scent of darkness.

She knew who she was. She knew what she wanted. She knew whom she wanted. She knew step by step how. How did she know?

Because the damn coma built a warrior in her, once a petrified heart covered with viscous empathy, pouring out feelings from the very core like a unicorn vomiting rainbows. She built her vision of the future, and in her future, there was only him.

Her faith in success was tested by the doubts. But who more than she could fall and then rise with greater strength?

Time to the goal? Patience.

Surely everyone would expect a simple fairy tale love, with a dreamy happy ending, but such stories actually happen rarely, let's face the truth and what perspective they would have. such love never, never happens. Why?

Because I believe that such love is then empty. It's only a superficial love, sweet sipping from each other's beaks without a deeper sense of getting to know the corners of the other person.

Such sweet knowing dooms us to an upstream defeat of being unaware of the potential hidden within the innermost parts of every human soul of each partner.

November 16th, a day of breakthrough but really, a day that marked the first day of a new reality for her inner strength, for her steel shield that cannot fall to the ground despite the blows dealt.

To see the rainbow, you must first endure the rain.

These words etched in her mind, like a mantra repeated to young children during the learning of speech, walking, and the first important daily tasks, all done with such inherent perfection only to ensure that they, when becoming adults, could hold their steel shield and never yield to the sea of empathy.

She never suspected that such a simple yet profoundly powerful sentence would imprint its ideology of understanding the world and the emotions surrounding her daily existence, much like the words spoken in profound mourning, "To never regret the dead, you must regret the living."

Though after all the experiences and trials, it's hard for her to understand this herself; there's a certain logic to it if you think about it for longer, for a person spends their whole life searching for the meaning of existence.

Did she ever contemplate what the future might look like while thinking about it one day? Could she have imagined what was just beginning to happen on this important November day, overshadowing her mundane daily duties at home? No! Why?

Because she had stopped thinking about the future, and the spark that flickered with every thought quickly extinguished because time was so cruel, and one had to seize the here and now. The battle had begun, so it was time to engage in the first fight.

She sat on the edge of her seat, staring at the screen of her phone as if it were a magical crystal ball that would reveal the course of events. She needed one small message, one little sound from her phone to momentarily calm her heart, which was racing a million times a minute as she read the message.

Suddenly. it's there! The sound, so long-awaited, so dreamed-of, and yet so different from the ones before. It seemed the same, yet different, magnificent because why? Full of unknowns. Because it could either shatter her heart into a million pieces or clothe her in the steel shield she had recently stashed in the closet, the one she had worn for so long.

Why? Why did she doubt herself and hide it away? Let's call it a momentary folly, and the sound and message she had just received reminded her how, despite momentary doubts, the truth remained that there is no end. No goodbyes, only love!

Is it not the moment to mention hope, to talk about all the things one believes in when belief is scarce? Because it was hope that helped her survive moments of horror when she thought everything was over, and hope took away the remnants of her superhuman imagination that perhaps not everything was lost.

The person who was recruited to be her eyes and ears in places where they couldn't be together had become her friend, someone who could fill the void in her heart, a place that was supposed to remain empty forever.

It found someone who could become important, someone who could fill the sadness of the space-time of lonely days and evenings with long conversations, really about nothing and everything. Who was he?

That must remain a secret because there are few people like him. An exceptional individual, lonely on his life's path, thirsty for love like few others. Searching but unable to find it.

What can we call him? An outstanding listener with extraordinary empathy. Nothing more, nothing less. That's all about him. Why? Because that's what the hell he wanted!

One, two, three. It was hard to believe, and yet she rubbed her eyes in amazement. She couldn't believe the message she had received. It was like a child looking under the Christmas tree on a holiday morning, waiting for that one dreamed-of, longed-for gift, wrapped in the most beautiful paper and tied with the most wonderful and shiny ribbon her eyes could see.

That's exactly how it was with her then, her eyes sparkled like the glow of holiday ribbons. A sight she couldn't even dream of. A photo! She saw a photo and froze. She allowed her eyes to shine with the brilliance of her tears. These were tears of happiness and emotion.

Joy and disbelief because it was his apartment that was adorned with gifts he had received from her. Photographs and presents, everything stood in the forefront like the best athlete on the podium, waiting to receive the golden, most important trophy of his life.

His actions were her greatest reward at that moment, her gold medal in the marathon that had just finished, and a taste of the triathlon that was just beginning. Everything was in its place, not only her gifts but also his behavior.

Because back when they wandered together through dreams in the cloudless moments of being together, her biggest goal was to make his life more family-oriented, to help him feel the greatness of spending time with loved ones because it doesn't take much to lose them.

It doesn't take much to never have the chance to see them again, to never feel the warmth of the touch of a loved one. It was a great surprise when she learned that his birthday had become the first moment of change in his attitude toward family.

It was a tribute that she interpreted without speaking to him, that she knew he did it because it mattered to her. That something that had no value for him had value for her. He did it because she knew that although he had tried to have a heart of stone toward her, love could break any hardness.

On that day, she saw not only photographs on shelves; she also saw the whole family he was trying to accommodate, just as she had taught him and most importantly, in all of this, SHE was not there.

She, the woman trying to replace her, was a source of pain and confusion for her. The question of who is better than her can be subjective, but in her heart, this competition didn't matter.

What hurt her was the fact that she had been replaced by someone else, that her love had been exchanged for a new one, using the classic strategy, 'the best way to get over an old love is to find a new one'.

However, this was a mistaken belief because attempting to quickly fall in love with someone new to erase memories of an old love often only led to complications.

On his birthday, when he should have been enjoying family celebrations, he went out with friends to celebrate. It would have been fine, except that she appeared there—too early to be at home with family, but already early enough to be present among friends and officially take her place by his side.

Her presence didn't suggest that she considered this day important or that she was interested in leaving any impression on others. She was supposed to replace her, but she shone by his side like the brightest star, which had been pushed off the pedestal by a gray mouse.

The report she received clearly indicated that she was only there in body, and it was also evident that she didn't feel comfortable, listening all evening to stories about his ex.

She was nothing more than a statistic at first, and later, as it turned out, a woman filling the nighttime void in his bed. Her heart bled more with each passing minute, but at the same time, she heated up with her determination to fight.

In her mind, there was not so much a plan as an unwavering resolve. Her determination to achieve her goal and get what she came for was stronger than the thought that he was currently kissing someone else.

She knew well that she was meant to play the role of nothing more than a remedy for a broken heart, but how do you heal a heart with someone who uncannily resembles the one from before?

The same shade of hair, like hot sand lying on the shore of a magnificent blue-lagoon coast, where the scent of a wonderful breeze hangs in the air, causing shivers on the skin with each stronger gust.

Height so perfect that, with a heightened sense of fear, she could immediately seek refuge in his safe embrace, figuratively speaking, fitting under his arm. Eyes like emeralds set in the most beautiful golden necklace, gleaming with every bend of a sunbeam.

A mouth that swallows you irretrievably, and depending on the falling light, changes its shade to a yellow resembling the menacing gaze of a cat from the most terrifying children's tale, which, from being a companion to a witch, has become a mythical terror for humanity.

The only, but also the most important difference between them was the style in which they presented themselves.

Despite her depressive experiences and battles for life, despite the changes her body went through as women with a double-beating heart under their breasts do, her presence was never flawed.

She loved to shine and draw attention to herself by her man's side, provoking not jealousy in him but in others. Because if she could express her thoughts with a look, she would probably have shouted, "Look but don't touch," more than once.

The pride emanating from her man's chest was a reflection of his feelings for her, of how beautiful and unique she was to him. And although her successor resembled her in many aspects, that significant difference in their styles emphasized the 'and', saying that they were like gold and metal.

Like unremarkable metal, blending into the crowd and never standing out with its shining details like gold.

Days and weeks passed, and they remained in contact. It couldn't be called a very close relationship, but in their case, simple message exchanges spoke volumes about the stages unfolding in their lives.

Shortly after his birthday, she—let's call her by the nickname we used earlier, the statistic. So, shortly after his birthday, the statistic was pushed to the background, and during meetings with his friends and her secret emissary, he repeatedly claimed that it was too early to talk about a comeback. Too early to draw conclusions about their future together, and certainly too early to make any decisions.

That was enough for her because too early certainly didn't mean it would never happen. It was her driving force in persevering toward her goal. Messages about everything and nothing elevated to a higher level, with one phone call per week.

A few minutes of connection gave her the energy to keep going, to keep fighting, and then it became a routine that, amid the daily duties of being a mom, served as an escape and hope that happiness would come soon. She didn't need much to feel his presence, even though he was far away from her.

Christmas was approaching, and she felt that their reunion was only a matter of time, that they would be together soon, and she would finally see the spark in his eyes when he looked at her.

She counted down to the New Year because as the oldest New Year's wishes say, "new year, new you, new changes, new time," that's how she envisioned the upcoming year.

Every evening before falling asleep, she dreamed up and created new scenarios for their future together. She even knew how to organize everything, so that their shared life would start like a blank white sheet in a new country, a new reality, new possibilities.

When on New Year's Eve, to her surprise, their message exchange turned into a photo report, she didn't expect to feel such relief in her heart. The certainty that surrounded her was no longer uncertainty and speculation:

Maybe she's there too? Maybe she's responding briefly? Maybe she sees me as a good friend?

No, none of those things! It became clear, almost as clear as the sun that their end had come shortly after his birthday. After all, which self-respecting woman could endure comparisons and talk about her ex?

She trembled at the mere thought that even though they were apart, they were entering the New Year together. That's why she dared to start a significant topic and decided to dig into it until she got the answer she hoped for.

With small steps, a bit shy yet quite straightforwardly, she told him how much she missed him, just as her daughter missed him, who not only heard from him frequently but also talked to him on the phone many times.

Her little darling saw how much joy this man brought her, so she decided to use it to convince him to meet sooner. She never, absolutely never, wanted her daughter to become a bargaining chip, and not many would think otherwise, but that was absurd.

She just knew how much he cared for her, and even though he could keep her at a distance and not show any feelings, he was simply touched and melted by that little creature, like milk chocolate exposed to the sun's rays beating too strongly against the car's windshield.

She didn't need to wait too many weeks; her patience wasn't tested for too long. He agreed faster than she could have imagined. She didn't know what guided his actions, she couldn't read it in his eyes or in the course of the conversation.

Why did he act this way? Was it the calm before the storm? In her mind, a few scenarios were forming. Perhaps it's a strategy on his part to come and go as quickly as possible, ending it definitively—no messages, no phone calls, no photos. The end, finito!

Perhaps he understood how much he misses her, how much he loves her daughter, and how much he wants to be with them again. Maybe it's time for an engagement?

However, none of these scenarios came to pass. During their first meeting after such a long time apart, it wasn't a natural encounter between two close people. It felt awkward, strange, and unbelievable that they were here and now together, with a whole weekend ahead of them.

And even though she had been waiting for this so eagerly, the sadness that accompanied her suddenly took on the same taste of bitterness and sorrow that she knew all too well.

All her insides buzzed like sour fruits because she didn't know how to behave, and she started to feel an internal sense of whether she really wanted this. Whether she hadn't become her own puppet in a game she had planned and devised.

She felt something akin to the saying, 'you want the cookie until you can't have the cookie', and when she almost had that cookie in her grasp, she felt boredom and the tastelessness of further effort and struggle.

The weekend turned out to be quite wonderful but also different from what she had anticipated and planned. It was rather chilly toward her, and to her surprise, he didn't show any interest or remnants of the feelings that could be lurking within him.

He invested all his energy and attention in her daughter, which, to her amazement, he seemed to connect with wonderfully despite language barriers and his limited experience with children.

However, she already knew at that time that this love story would not find its happy ending. Even though he had restored her strength and hope, she increasingly felt that this man was not the one meant for her.

She loved him with an immense love. The sacrifices she made were almost unimaginable, and she herself didn't know she had such depths of feelings to bestow upon others. So, what could have gone wrong when both of them were present?

When both of them could have had a conversation about their future, not as a couple, but as acquaintances? When both of them were aware of their flaws and expectations and could clearly define their future.

They didn't do it, and it wasn't because they lacked courage; it was due to a completely different, yet quite prosaic reason. They simply lost interest in each other. Love didn't fade; they just seemed to have stopped seeing in each other the people they were when they first met.

Prolonged separation, the possibility of meeting other people, had blurred their idealized view of themselves. They didn't give up and continued to maintain contact, planning increasingly bold trips together.

One of the trips was even successful, but it lacked the most important thing—the one that binds two people, stripping them of their intimacy.

They lacked the shedding of mutual taboos, the intimacy, and tenderness. There were no kisses or gestures of affection to signify the passionate, fiery love they once shared, where they wanted to show it at every opportunity.

At this point, they were just ordinary people, ordinary friends spending time together, a couple where only one was making an effort, and the other was a passive participant in this poorly planned battle for their relationship.

Neither of them attempted to salvage the remains of what could have been in this rapidly sinking swamp, and neither had a clue about what to do to make things different. His gaze remained empty and as dark as the abyss into which she had once sunk.

He was no longer her beacon of hope; that hope was never supposed to exist. He had become a hazy memory, within arm's reach yet out of touch. They didn't end it because neither of them knew how; deep down, maybe both hoped that somehow everything would work out, and they'd emerge unscathed without much effort, and this would all be just a big joke.

They waited, unaware that everything was about to change soon. Tough times were about to descend, not just for them but for the entire world. Now, everything was going to change, and they were oblivious to the fact that their paths would no longer cross.

They bid farewell at the station, like a mother kissing her son goodbye before he set off on a school trip with his friends, expecting his return home soon.

If she had known then that it would be the last time she'd touch his face, the last time she'd smell his skin, the last time she'd gaze into the depths of his eyes, that she'd never have a chance to ignite that abyss and bring forth the light, she would have played it differently.

Pandemic

A big bang. Mid-March, no one expected it. Global isolation, where even someone who was lonely would remain so for a long time. The only source of contact with another person would be through various carriers, whether by phone or online.

Going to the store, not only to buy essential supplies but to establish human connections, would become impossible. Being alone during this difficult time was like an invitation to enter a state of depression.

Fortunately, she wasn't alone; she had her beloved daughter with whom she could spend every moment during the prolonged isolation, without sharing her with anyone else. They were each other's whole world, friends, and confidantes, everyday companions.

The lack of the need to leave home for work or daycare also revealed another wonderful aspect of motherhood to her. She felt something she had always known, but now it intensified her desire.

A big, wonderful family, many children, and many wonderful family moments, not just during the holidays around a big table, but every day.

Even as the days passed, all looking the same, and the situation with the epidemic continued to grow in strength— a force that was reaping a harvest of human tragedy and countless tears—the overwhelming pain accompanied her at every step.

The mere thought that he might be out there somewhere, that so many things could have been different during their last encounter, caused her tremendous anguish.

Her mind was a whirlwind of thoughts, filled with plans for redemption, unrealized desires, and unspoken words. How could she make things right? How could she change the course of events?

These questions remained unanswered for a long time. She had to settle for doing what was possible in the given situation and moment. She had to move forward blindly on a path illuminated by countless fantasies.

Without hesitation, she made one last attempt to reignite the old flames of emotion. She believed that the solitude everyone experienced due to the isolation could sustain their telephone relationship.

She thought that by calling and writing, she could awaken unforgettable feelings within him, making his heart resonate with hers like a massive brass bell, causing goosebumps to appear on her skin.

Weeks went by, but with each subsequent gesture she made toward him, she encountered greater resistance. The sound of his voice, resonating through the phone's receiver, no longer brought pleasure.

Her pounding heart, waiting for the tones of an incoming call, stirred a bubbling sensation in her stomach. When her heart had fallen in love with him, the feeling she experienced in her body was a mythical sensation known to people as 'butterflies in the stomach'.

However, what she felt now certainly did not resemble the feelings she had experienced back then. It was more like seething lava, piercing and scorching every fiber of her being.

She became increasingly aware of how close everything was to falling apart. She was more aware of it than ever before. For the first time in a very long while, she stopped deceiving herself.

She faced the truth and understood that it would never be the same as it was on the first day. It wouldn't be like the first few weeks or months. She realized that fate had prepared a completely different path for her.

However, her awareness greatly diverged from her actions. One logical explanation was missing for what had truly driven her at that time. What was truly smoldering in her mind remained a mystery.

It's been over three months since the world began to function quite differently. Three months in which everything that had been her stability in recent years changed.

Three months in which she had to put on a brave face to ensure that none of her loved ones realized that she was falling apart, that her heart had shattered into a million pieces. What mattered most was that her little spark didn't notice that she had a sad mom.

She did everything to keep their domestic happiness intact, even though her heart bled as if pierced by the sharpest sword. She knew that soon she would have to return to her professional life, that soon she would have to face reality.

Step out of her four walls, which had always been her sanctuary and refuge from the world around her. Home was the place where she felt safe.

Everything seemed to be quite different without him, without the ability to contact him. Her only link and news about him came from a mysterious acquaintance who was also increasingly distanced from him and from what was happening in his world.

Everything that could improve her mood was becoming increasingly distant, fading into the endless abyss of the unknown. For unknown reasons, contact with him started to resemble a receding mist in which thoughts wandered.

Their acquaintance dissolved like a gust of wind, a gust that couldn't gather strength. A gust that couldn't blow away all the unspoken words. It was the force behind their separation, turning them into strangers.

Together with the departure of her love, the connection faded, a connection that, over time, seemed to have no chance of survival, even though they sometimes spoke without words.

July arrived—considered the warmest month of the year. A time for trips and summer flings with newly made acquaintances. As one chapter closed, she didn't expect that something new would knock on her door from the back entrance.

Not as deep and genuine as she would have wished for, but something that at least, in a small way, helped her function without sadness and tears in her eyes. Her broad thoughts were often diverted onto a different path because someone new had captured her attention, someone who had never been on her list of dreams.

Despite the inner promises she made to herself that if fate was clearly indicating that love wasn't meant for her, she would wholeheartedly devote herself to her daughter.

However, the time she had to spend alone, far from him, hurt her so deeply that it caused frustration and loneliness. She surrendered once again to what fate had in store for her. Her damned subconscious mind once again plunged into the abyss of passion and desire, hoping to find happiness.

Returning to work turned out to be more surprising and unpredictable than even the greatest science fiction writer could have imagined. On the very first day, a big surprise awaited her.

Despite the attire that forced people to cover themselves entirely for fear of being infected by the unpredictable virus that wreaked havoc worldwide, she could still captivate with charm and undeniable allure.

Was it this that caught the attention of someone who, just a few months ago, wasn't even within her scope of interest? She didn't know herself. However, her remarkable perceptiveness could discern what the ordinary human eye couldn't.

Her exceptional ability to unleash a million words per minute without any significant pause made even the most embittered person become an extraordinary conversation partner.

And although her heart desired more, although her heart yearned for greater adoration, and though her body called for more, to her surprise, reason won the internal battle. She could say goodbye when everything was just starting to unfold, when she decided that she didn't want it to last longer.

Many women would feel like princesses being treated the way this newly met man treated her. However, their multiple encounters didn't make her feel the magic of passion and affection that could have lasted forever, or at least for a long time.

She only felt her free time being filled, and the excitement of her phone vibrating with his messages. His gentlemanly behavior toward her, instead of bringing her closer to him, pushed her further away.

She had always longed for it, for adoration, for flowers for no reason, for everything he did, but not from him. Perhaps that's why his efforts were in vain. Feeling frustrated for not showing him appreciation for his gestures, she decided to end it quickly and painlessly, like tearing off a band-aid.

Nothing could be more misleading because this knight in shining armor, who rode on a white horse, didn't give up as quickly as she wished. She wanted peace, closure, to shut the door tightly. However, he didn't allow her to do that with his possessiveness and stubbornness.

One summer evening, which usually changed the course of events, the knight who fought, even though he had forgotten his sword, began to surrender and give up this uneven battle for her heart.

Her heart, which had been stoned again because her thoughts were wandering around him, the one who pulled her out of the abyss. But he had become so inaccessible and distant that her thoughts, revolving around him, no longer caused pain but only brought fear.

Fear for herself and for what could happen to her life if she allowed herself to get lost in that bottomless pit.

How it usually happens in life, when he decided to let her go, her heart started thinking more and more about him. She was thinking about the knight who fought for her. The height of her emotional wall was insurmountable for him.

If one were to believe in the beliefs she had always held, the force watching over her wouldn't allow what was smoldering within her to come out.

The pain associated with it would be another unbearable blow to her fragile and bottomless being. The man who tried to win her heart with his appearance was the worst version of a modern man.

His divided attention among different women at the same time was something no one could accept, certainly not her. It had to end here and now, so she could begin to live. No more searching and believing she would be found.

That she would meet someone who would love her with all the life's mess, with all the demons that accompanied her every day and that emerged from the closet at the least expected moments like uninvited guests.

Someone who would love her daughter as strongly as the strike of Thor's mythical golden hammer from a distant galaxy. She decided to proceed this way and started living only for herself and her daughter, considering what had happened to her in recent weeks as a lesson.

For what is written to a person, as the saying goes, is like shit left on the road. She stopped searching and started believing.

Slide Six

On a certain August night, as she eagerly awaited the longed-for ritual of falling stars, contemplating her thoughts and wishes, she wondered why she deserved such a fate.

What causes divine judgments, where one person is marked in their existence by nothing but kindness and success, while another struggles with constant life failures? Why, sinking into this melancholic and contemplative mood, did she allow herself to ask such questions?

After all, her life is full of success; perhaps not perfect or ideal, but certainly colorful. For several years, it has been filled with the love of her child. Because, indeed, this is the most beautiful and purest form of love.

The one that expects nothing in return, the one that fills a person with pride, and the one that is the essence of human existence on this earthly plane. Love that is expressed in a child's eyes through the tiniest gestures, a love that no one or nothing else can replace.

Being the foundation of safety and belonging for someone made her finally understand her purpose. Though her dreams, etched into her subconscious, remained unfulfilled, she allowed what was planned for her from above to be sent her way.

Filled with hope, about which she had conflicting opinions not long ago, it entered her life like a daily routine. Prayers to hope, to the one that didn't exist, to the one that applauded her existence, to the one that must exist because hope is what makes us want to get up every day.

She also got back on her feet, piecing together all the small fragments of her scattered life. She placed her trust in herself and her child, focusing on their happiness. She embraced the most wonderful moments of life while also realizing how fragile it can be.

We often make the mistake of thinking we have all the time in the world, but time is the most ruthless force humanity has encountered. Because anyone who believes that death is the world's executioner is greatly mistaken.

Death comes swiftly, takes what it wants, and departs without looking back. Time, on the other hand, always remains, a belief and sorrow that there could have been more done.

We yearn for moments when we could have seized an opportunity to do something we dreamed of but lacked the strength and courage to execute. Time is merciless, and it cannot be reversed. Time will not wait. Time flows so inexorably that before we know it, what we cared about is gone.

She understood this difference, knowing that tomorrow might not provide a chance to fill her mind with memories. She decided to take action, to give her daughter and herself the power of memories and experiences.

However, fate had other plans for her once again. Once again, she thought that fate wanted to mock her and put her strength to the test.

Rose-Colored Glasses

Looking at the world through rose-colored glasses is nothing more than envisioning reality in a different dream. Idealizing something we constantly dream about. She began to believe that her view through rose-colored glasses was becoming more than just a fantasy.

When you stop searching for happiness, it finds you on its own. It seeks a path to you even through closed doors. Even then, it finds that small gap through which it can break through and reach your heart, enlarging it every day.

Because when darkness falls, when every small piece of your being drifts into irrevocable darkness, you wait and dream for someone to rescue you from the abyss of that soulless agony.

Your body silently descends into the abyss that remains in your heart. Defeated by your own naivety and greed for something that perhaps should never have belonged to you. She watches as familiar faces walk away, embraced by the love of another person's arms.

She envies the tenderness lavished upon that woman. She gazes at the idealized beauty of pure love without scratches or scars.

That day, that night, she had no idea that it would change her entire life. Not just her life but THEIR life. As the summer wind whispered its soothing sounds, she immersed her lips in another glass of her favorite red wine.

Each sip brought about a strange sense of something impending, much to her surprise. She remembered having a dream on several recent nights, a dream about a man who resembled someone she saw in her future.

For a moment, forgetting about her daily worries, she lost herself in the friendly embrace of a relaxed evening, scrolling through mindless internet memes, eventually reaching its depths.

It was then that someone wrote. Someone who bore a striking resemblance to the same figure from her dreams. Eyes of a laser-blue color, surrounded by a fan of long, dark, and curled lashes. Lips with a pale pink hue, visibly soft, which enveloped with their delicate kisses.

Immersing herself in the depths of his human appearance, everything seemed drawn like that of a Greek god sent to Earth. Not excessively drawn, with each muscle defined and sculpted, centimeter by centimeter, worked out with hours of dedication.

The overall look was completed with a hairstyle that varied depending on preferences and circumstances, styled for visual pleasure. At times, it was brushed straight over his forehead, almost touching his heavenly azure eyes, and other times, it was swept back, adhering to the refined and elegant style.

If sophistication and charm were to accompany his demeanor, he could be considered an ideal. An ideal with secrets and a past drawn like the most sensuous multivolume novel. At first, there were timid but inviting overtures.

Hey, nice photo.
Liked the post.
Liked the post.
Liked the post.

And so, after a few weeks, a breakthrough occurred. Their conversation, initially resembling nothing more than the exchange of words between two six-year-olds, slowly evolved into a spinning carousel.

A carousel with wagons that alternated between boasting and sharing daily adventures. He was a man who couldn't stay in one place, constantly wandering and seeking pleasures and fantasies. Hooking up with a different girl he met, forgetting about her by the next morning.

Reveling in his not-so-glorious reputation as a ladies' man. So, what drew her to him? What made her give him her time and interest when their life perspectives represented quite extreme visions of life?

But before that happened, several months passed, as time likes to surprise us. In their acquaintance, they often attracted each other and then she pushed him away. Then there was attraction again, followed by her pushing him away, sometimes even withholding contact for weeks.

Yet, he persisted incessantly. Was it due to his desire to add her to his list of conquests? Or did he simply feel something for her that he hadn't felt for any woman in a long time?

Although it remained a mystery for a long time, one thing wasn't a secret—their conversations often took on a playful tone akin to the banter between teenagers.

I love misunderstandings written in rhyme, we just need a spear and a woman to sum up the circus where one monkey was missing but there was a clown and a queen (yesterday snow, today Snow White); he liked her, she tossed him aside, at the end of this story, the spell broke because in a fairy tale, it's about the ending, and not everything always ends well, will you allow the same to happen with them?

I will cross mountains, forests, valleys, and at the end of this journey, there will be a cottage, and inside it, the unknown will happen. I will enter there, close my eyes, and say a spell, and soon, a miracle will happen.

A cottage and inside it, the unknown, and everything that will be in it. You will appear opposite, holding poison in your hands. I will approach, take it from you, disappear, leaving a clue on how to find me.

When you find me and we return to the place where I met you, the cottage will be back in the same place, and we will continue to discover the unknown inside it.

In the moonlit night, when darkness covered the sky's last glimmers of hope, she saw a tiny light. Dreaming of a falling star, she thought this little light was heading toward her, but it turned out to be something else, something more unexpected.

At first, she couldn't reach it because her height was no more than an average Michelin-sized little person. At the top of a tree, something stopped that shouldn't have been there, but the power of her desires reached it.

From the nutshell of a tiny stardust pebble emerged the voice of a green little person, ready for a fight with a raised sword. In their sarcastic existence, the battle of equals among these little people began to demand greater communication to return together to a planet so distant that the average human mind lags behind light-years.

Each day, the green little people discovered something new and more surprising. The fear among the little people of themselves was so great that only one option remained; a joint journey within the pervasive darkness.

Did they attempt it? The fairy tale continues, moving to a very prosaic and clichéd place, 'beyond the forests and hills'.

And though it sounded funny, and they often joked and swapped fairy tales between them, her story still revolved around darkness. The more they wrote and talked, the more it fit into her daily routine.

It melded with her, like heated wax into darkness. Both of them were getting more and more absorbed in this connection. He often emphasized that she was the only woman in his life, that the past and the stories he told about himself in their many phone conversations were just that—the past.

He convinced her that only she and only with her did he love to talk. She believed him, and then, like a bolt from the blue, a thought struck her like a head-on collision with a wall. How could this happen? How could fate allow her to end up in the same situation again?

Déjà vu—suddenly, she's in a car, telling a recently met man about her past and that she's not alone in the world.

Tears stream down her cheeks, and she battles with her thoughts, hearing only a deaf, empty echo in the headset.

Silence, that bottomless silence, which left its mark on her soul, returned to her like a ball ricocheting. Fear, pain, anxiety, a rollercoaster of emotions flowed beneath her skin as that silence continued mercilessly.

Then she heard his breath, heralding the long-awaited release of some kind of response. What was she hoping for? What was she waiting for? What did she want? Nothing! She was prepared for rejection and the likely end of this connection.

She had thoroughly prepared herself for the discontinuation of what had promised to be so magical, almost unreal. She knew that according to scientific studies conducted worldwide, more than seventy-five percent of men do not want to commit to a woman with a child.

Accustomed to fate playing cruel tricks on her, she was convinced that this one belonged to the group of those who, according to science, did not want to commit. After a moment of silence following another deep breath, it came, "I need to think about it, I'll call you in the evening."

The uttered sentence echoed in her phone's receiver, foreshadowing what she knew when she came up with this idea. Why did she want to tell him? Why didn't she continue the phone flirting?

Was this seemingly insignificant thing about to turn into something else because she started feeling something for him? Or did she just want to remain honest with him because she was the happiest mom of the most wonderful girl in the world?

Subconsciously, she felt that she had to get it out, that her little secret was not something to hide or be ashamed of, that not talking about it wouldn't protect it from the world's evils. That hiding it might make him see it differently someday.

That day, she had to pick herself up and get a grip because experiencing another mourning for a potential love lost had become as mundane as daily bread to her. A few hours of sadness, a few hours of crying, a few self-pitying evenings, and boom, it was over.

After sharing what she had done on her way to work with her friends, opinions were divided. The majority gave little chance of him calling in the evening. The same gratitude believed, in her conviction that his persistence and desire to conquer and tick off conquests on his list would prevail.

She respected them for not sugarcoating things, for their honesty, and at the same time, she was slowly forming her own opinion of him. A day filled with so many emotions and so many unspoken words could only end in one way. She, wine, a book.

Shortly after twenty-second hour, her phone began to vibrate, and his name appeared on the display. The whirlwind of thoughts she had in her head, along with her trembling hands, was so intense that she wasn't sure if she had the strength to hear what he had to say.

She wondered why he was calling and why he wanted to tell her the same thing—that nothing would come of it, that he was angry, that she had hidden it from him, and that she had wasted a few months of his life that he could have spent on someone without maternal obligations.

The scream in her head told her that it would be better if he acted like many other guys and simply stopped contacting her after revealing the truth. It was too much for her.

Hurtful words carved into her spark hurt her the most. However, fate had something different in store for her this time, different from before; it decided to treat her differently.

"Hello?"

"Well, hey," it sounded from his mouth.

The echo on her side of the line was deafening, waiting for what was inevitable. One, two, three, let him say it already, and let both of them get it off their chests and move forward.

"I behaved like an idiot. I'm sorry. I shouldn't have ended the conversation like that after what you told me. I needed to sort everything out in my head. Tell me about your daughter, what's her name?"

She stood frozen, in that very second, someone poured a bucket of cement on her, which was just beginning to harden. Was he trying to tell her that he was serious about her? That what had connected them was real and sincere? That he was taking her with the whole package?

Or had she become just another challenge and conquest on his list? So many unknowns were now flooding her mind. So many fears began to take center stage.

However, she found the strength in herself to look at everything clearly and objectively from the sidelines, like a third person listening to this love story.

Their much-anticipated first meeting wasn't coming off easily as they continued planning and offering excuses from her side.

This November night brought many unexpected things. She had decided that she didn't want any relationships, that she was devoting too many thoughts to what he truly meant to her and whether he was planning to have fun at her expense.

However, she was so committed and so eager for everything they had talked about to come true that she put everything on one card. She decided to meet him and never think about him again.

It was supposed to end with this very weekend in December. Their paths were supposed to diverge, not giving him the satisfaction of having her on his list of conquests. Full of worries and concerns, she headed to their meeting, fearing that at the last moment he would change his mind and leave her to the whims of fate in this unknown city.

She was afraid that at the last moment, when he saw her from a distance, he would turn and run away faster than lightning. Sweat was running down her back as she walked through the airport parking lot to the place where they were supposed to meet.

She saw him from afar, and her heart began to beat wildly as she felt foolish and irresponsible. How could he turn out to be a serial killer who had easily lured her to him? She was afraid that for the next three days, she would be stuck with him, and what if, after the first hour, it turned out that face-to-face conversations were not as natural and stress-free for them as they had thought?

What would she do if he said goodbye in just a few moments? She walked with all her fears, seeing that there were less than ten steps left to him, wondering now how to greet him.

Should she shake his hand, hug him, or maybe it would be best to drop dead on the sidewalk right now? She laughed in her thoughts at her silly ideas, while also silently begging fate to have a little wine for her, which she had asked for when she was still on her way.

Talking to him through text messages was much easier, so she didn't hesitate to ask him right away, expressing without any reservations that she was very stressed about this meeting.

Two small wine bottles on her lap and a photo sent to her friends, who at that time were sharing their amorous excitements with him. The caption under the photo spoke for itself, "The flowers of a modern woman," which was humorous but surprisingly true.

After an hour-long car journey filled with singing, as if at a karaoke night in a roadside pub, they arrived at his house, where she had to freshen up quickly, and then they both headed to a party at his friends' place.

Steep wooden stairs led straight to his bedroom, and her first thought was that she wasn't the first. The doors opened, revealing black and white striped bedding forming a pattern of geometric rectangles.

Her thoughts were more troubling than anything else, convinced of how many women had been there before her and how many of them had been treated just as she intended to treat herself this weekend.

So many negative emotions swirled within her as she looked at the place where she would spend the next few days.

Her surprise was even greater when he showed no interest and didn't exhibit any tangible passion. She knew it then. He saw her, and everything in him extinguished. He saw her, and he knew he couldn't just send her away.

He knew her return ticket was two days away, and he had to spend that time with her. It was too apparent and emphasized by him. Both the party and the entire weekend quickly passed, despite her earlier fears and exaggerated feelings.

He didn't allow her to feel uncomfortable in his company and in his home. They spent the entire Saturday afternoon and every free moment on moments of ecstasy and passion, savoring each minute together.

Because as she knew, this time was their last, she had no idea what was going on in his mind and how he saw it. And although in many ways, she felt embarrassed about her body in front of him, even though she had no reason to be embarrassed, remembering every single conversation where he told her about other women.

Their splendors and curves had triggered some complexes in her about her own body. However, this was soon to end, and what he might say about her would no longer matter to her. She came, she conquered, and she left.

That was supposed to be her motto. After all, how could you be with someone for whom the measure of manhood and respect among others was about how much, how often, and where?

As she got out of the car, she was already counting the minutes until she would see her daughter again. She counted, believing that what had just happened was one big adventure.

If she ever had the opportunity to tell her friends that she knows exactly what they're talking about because she experienced a one-night stand herself.

A weekend adventure that had to end with a quick farewell, perhaps a gentle kiss in remembrance of a successful experience, or at most, a friendly hug. Everything was pointing to a new beginning in this surprising ending of their acquaintance.

"I LOVE YOU," he whispered in her ear, gently brushing her skin with the pale pink cushions of his lips.

Slide Seven

Three deep breaths, and everything still whirls in her head. After all, these are the most beautiful words in the world. These are words you don't just throw around or say to anyone.

These are words worth more than a hundred gold bars. Beautiful words but oh, so fragile in their meaning. Taught by experience, she had to keep her cool and explain to her mind in a rational way what had just happened in that parking lot.

What was the intention behind those words? When considering all the events of the past weekend logically, he got everything he could have wanted. He had no reason to lure her to him with those words.

So, did he want to make her journey back home more pleasant, so she wouldn't feel like a complete stranger? That would be exceptionally strange and irrational on his part, and he would only cast himself in a negative light by doing so, simply because he had never experienced real love and didn't understand the weight and power of the words he had spoken.

She hoped this wouldn't occupy her mind any further, and with the end of the trip, this story would come to an end as well.

Puk, puk, her phone vibrates shortly after turning it on, and she has a full sense of unease that this isn't a message from her friends checking in or hurrying her for a quicker summary of the past seventy-two hours.

Instead, it's a message from him. A message filled with concern and affection. A message that just threw her entire plan out the window because, along with her response to his caring text, all the strength to keep him at bay vanished.

No one really knows what was the ignition point of this love story, whether it was the words 'I love you' or the sign that, with her return and their separation, his interest didn't diminish but only grew stronger.

These were no longer the conversations and exchanges of messages between two people planning to perhaps meet again for another adventurous weekend. These were the conversations of two people whose lives had already begun to intertwine, two people who couldn't get enough of each other and dedicated every spare moment to each other.

Even routine gatherings with friends happened together with them, despite the thousands of kilometers between them. Their feelings for each other grew stronger, and the surge of their emotions repeatedly reminded her that she hadn't reciprocated with the same words she had received from him.

She was afraid that everything was happening too fast and was too beautiful, and it might crumble and fall apart like a house of cards at any moment. The nagging thought that a man like him, independent, handsome, and most importantly, without family commitments, could genuinely fall in love with her, was always on her mind.

To dedicate his hard-earned life in the world of single women to her, who had already been marked by life experiences more than many people in their prime—it seemed strange.

Their planned New Year's Eve meeting was inevitably accelerated by global events. The epidemic gained strength, returning at the least expected moment, and struck with such force that death reaped a harvest of its own and feasted for all time.

Fate decided for her, as she wondered whether New Year's Eve would be a good time for him to meet her daughter. Now, she had to make a quick decision about whether she could afford an uninvited guest before the holiday season, someone who would stay with her until the New Year.

Her thoughts twisted through unbearably painful turns until she finally made a decision and put everything on one card. After all, the world was closing down, and human interactions would be limited for an unknown duration.

She reminded herself that she was just one of many women he could choose from, yet he expended an incredible amount of strength and money to reach her before everything was locked down.

His actions provided her with the first crucial evidence that she had taken up residence in his heart so strongly that nothing and no one could remove her from that place. Cheers and hugs, kisses and conversations until dawn as they stood before her door.

She was full of apprehension, wondering how this first meeting would look for both her daughter and herself. This meeting was with someone with whom she had shared her life and planned dreams and a future for weeks, not knowing that what they had imagined would soon become their reality.

The New Year, another New Year, when she forms her mantra in her thoughts. New year, new me, new dreams, new plans, new goals. However, she didn't realize how accurate her thoughts were this time.

Just a few moments separated her from something that would change their lives forever. She didn't suspect that she would hear something like this after such a short time of knowing him.

He couldn't imagine life without her, couldn't imagine building a relationship and a family with her from a distance, without beating around the bush, he asked directly about living together.

Yes, at that moment, he was already so determined and well-thought-out that he was willing to throw away everything he had built and achieved for her. Their love was so strong that he couldn't provide a greater proof of his love at that moment.

Packing up so many years of his life and coming here? Here, to the woman behind whom there would always be someone else? Someone who is the father of her child? And someone with whom she shared a piece of her unpleasant history?

He was brave to take on all this mess of nothingness she had created here. He loved her above all else, loved her daughter above all else, often repeating to her that she was a part of her mom, and he loved her mom the most in the world.

They made such a wonderful couple that the most beautiful love story could compete with them. However, the reality that was prepared for them showed that the world is not painted through rose-colored glasses, and her strength lies in faith, not giving up the hope she found, surviving the storm, and waiting for the rainbow.

New Reality

Looking back like an echo of everything that surrounds us in the rearview mirror of the car, she didn't want to look there.

She didn't want to go back to the ruins of her past when now a new reality had dawned. When everything unfolded so surprisingly quickly that it didn't leave her a moment to think.

Could it be that what she had been waiting for so many years was now beginning in her life?

She used to think that you could only truly fall in love once in life. She knew how wrong she was believing in this theory. You can love multiple times because each love is different and each marks a person in a different way.

Each love leaves a different woven basket of experiences and memories. These memories are sometimes gray, hazy, and painful, and sometimes, they are dressed in the most beautiful rainbow-colored blanket.

Every experience she gained taught her something different and, most importantly, allowed her to explore the corners of her own mind. She could love and feel. She could make choices, sometimes better, sometimes worse.

She could forgive, and she could love with a strength that not everyone can find within themselves. What is happening in her life now, will it bring her the long-awaited contentment and fulfillment?

She feared that reality would stop being painted in rose-colored glasses, and what was planned for her would be an extraordinarily large rollercoaster, like the biggest one in an amusement park.

She was sinking. She was sinking in a sea of tears, drowning in her own humiliation, sinking, knowing that her life was no longer the struggle of two people. Now, it's the struggle of three beings and she wasn't talking about the kind of fight that involved HIM.

Yes! Another child was born into her world and she gazed into the darkness of the past, gazed into the depths of hidden feelings, and knew what a great mistake she had made.